PROVIDENCIA

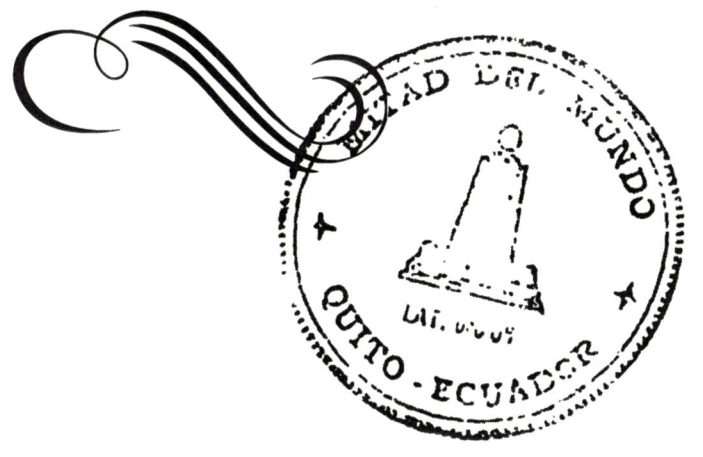

by DEBORAH A. HODGE

Divine Inspiration Publishing

©Copyright 2014 by Deborah A. Hodge. Printed and bound in the United States of America. All rights reserved. No part of this book may be reproduced or transmitted in any form or by any means, electronic or mechanical, including photocopying, recording, or by an information storage and retrieval system – with the exception of a reviewer who may quote brief passages in a review to be printed in a newspaper, magazine, or e-zine without written permission from the publisher. For information, contact Divine Inspiration Publishing, PO Box 210414, Auburn Hills, MI 48326. 800/515-3770.

This book is a work of fiction. All characters are fictional. Any resemblance to persons living or dead is purely coincidental.

Scripture quotations are taken from the THE HOLY BIBLE, NEW INTERNATIONAL VERSION®, NIV® Copyright © 1973, 1978, 1984, 2011 by Biblica, Inc.® Used by permission. All rights reserved worldwide..

Interior Design and Layout by Divine Inspiration Publishing

Edited by Leah Maurer, Editing with Purpose

Visit our websites at www.divineinspirationpublishing.com and
ISBN-978-0-9820490-0-6
1 2 3 4 5 6 7 8 9 10
✝
First Edition

ATTENTION CHURCHES, CHRISTIAN ORGANIZATIONS, LIBRARIES: Quantity discounts are available on bulk purchases of this book for churches, fundraisers, book clubs or childrens' groups. For information, please contact Divine Inspiration Publishing, PO Box 210414 Auburn Hills, MI 48326; (800)515-3770

Dedication

To my brother, Barry whose faith has become sight, I miss you Brother Dear.

Jason could hear the distress in Sarah's voice. "You have accepted the call to the little church in Iowa, haven't you?"

Jason dropped his head and nodded yes.

"Is there any way you might be wrong about God's leading?"

He raised his head, stood erect and silent for a moment as he scanned her face for clues. The deep sadness he discovered caused his blood pressure to drop and his heart to hurt. He shifted and slowly shook his head.

He watched as Sarah shut her eyes in an attempt to stall a flood of emotion. She swallowed hard and forced another question. "Are you absolutely sure?"

He knew he had to be honest and hold nothing back. He gathered his strength, sighed and confessed as tenderly as he could, "I'm sure."

Tears trickled from her eyes and glistened as they ran down her face. "I don't know what to do."

Jason pulled her into his arms. She buried her face in his chest and sobbed. He hugged her tightly. "Sarah, we both know what we have to do. We just don't like it."

She nodded and sobbed some more. He didn't say anything. He just held her and stroked her hair as she cried. Finally, she spoke. "I just don't understand. It doesn't make any sense that God would bring us together only to separate us now."

"I know," he whispered.

She raised her head, sniffed to clear her nose, swallowed hard, and looked him directly in the eyes. "Could we really have been that wrong

Chapter 1

about us?" As she finished, she realized he was choking back tears.

"Maybe we were."

Sarah backed away. "What do you mean by that? Don't you love me anymore? Don't you want to marry me?"

"Sure I do, but it's not that simple. I wish it were."

Sarah put her hand to her chest and tried to catch her breath as she wrestled with his words. "What's that supposed to mean?"

Jason struggled to be strong. "We both know that being in the center of God's will is the most important thing in life."

Trembling and with tears streaming again, she nodded slowly and sighed, "Yeah ."

"For me being in the center in God's will means a church in Iowa, for you it means the hospital in Ecuador. I wish it weren't so, but we both know it is."

Sarah closed her eyes, sniffed again, and asked, "But where does that leave us?"

He shook his head. "I don't know."

Sarah bit her lip. "What if we never see each other again?"

He felt a tortured look take over his face. "We have to put all of that in God's hands."

He spewed out the words. "God, I can't believe it has been four years since we parted. You know I've tried to give it all to you, but thoughts of Sarah have crept into my mind and dreams this whole time. I have preached trust in You and surrender to Your will, all the while feeling like a failure concerning Sarah. I have struggled with it constantly. Now I am struggling with it again, especially since I am going to Ecuador, and there is a slight possibility that I will see her again.

"I don't have a choice — because of Professor Cohen's illness and surgery I am now the professor in charge of the mission practicum. The trip to Ecuador is ten days away and I am afraid about what might lie ahead. I have prayed continuously about it, but Lord I need to confide in my friend."

Providencia   *Deborah A. Hodge*

Jason swallowed hard, rubbed his face and shifted in his chair as he waited for his friend and colleague, Tom Barkley. He prayed once more. "Father, you know how apprehensive I am about this whole thing. Please use Tom to give me a new perspective." He felt a brief sense of relief just as he heard the squeaking of the door that signaled Tom's arrival.

Tom dropped his briefcase beside his desk and stuck out his hand. "Hello Jay."

Jason forced a smile and shook his hand. "Hi Tom."

"Sorry to keep you waiting."

"It's fine. I'm just glad we can talk."

Tom walked to his office fridge. "Anytime. Would you like something to drink?"

Jason shook his head. "No thanks."

Tom reached into the fridge for a bottle of water.

"Are you sure? I have plenty."

"I'm sure," Jason answered. Though he worked hard to control his emotions, his face mirrored his inner turmoil.

Tom sat down without opening his water. "What's up?"

Jason swallowed, took a deep breath and plunged in. "It's the mission trip."

"Logistical problems?"

Jason shook his head again. "No. Personal problems."

Tom set his water down, took off his glasses, sat down and put his elbows on the desk, and gave Jason his full attention. "What kind of personal problems?"

Jason chewed on his lip as he stared at the floor a moment before he answered. "Sarah Barnes."

Tom echoed, "Sarah Barnes."

"Sarah was my fiancée, and she's in Ecuador."

Tom stoked his chin, "So that's the personal problem?"

Chapter 1

Jason nodded and looked down.

"I can see how torn up you are. Why don't you tell me about it?"

Jason nodded without looking up.

"She's the girl I was sure I was going to marry."

"So what happened?"

Jason looked up. His brow was furrowed and his eyes signaled the depth of his pain. "God led us apart."

With wide-eyed confusion, Tom repeated, "God led you apart."

The furrow in Jason's brow deepened, his jaw tightened, and he swallowed hard. He nodded. "He did."

Tom shook his head as he sat back in his chair. "You'll have to explain that." He folded his hands and put them to his mouth as he listened to Jason's explanation.

"I met Sarah my senior year in college. It was love at first sight for me. It took her a little longer, but we both were convinced God was leading us toward marriage. I bought a ring and asked her to marry me. She said yes. We were making plans for the wedding and our future when everything changed. "Tom moved forward in his chair. "How?"

"She finished her nursing degree, passed her boards and was praying about what God would have her do and where. I was finishing my seminary degree and praying about my place of service. Almost simultaneously, God opened up a position for her in Ecuador and one for me in Iowa. We prayed, sought godly counsel, but we couldn't reconcile God's leadership in our lives. She was convinced He was leading her to Ecuador, and I was convinced He was leading me to Iowa. We were both deeply committed to obeying God even though we didn't understand why He was leading as He was. Consequently, she went to Ecuador, and I went to Iowa."

Tom shifted in his chair. "I see. How long has it been since you've seen her?"

"Four years."

Tom's eyes widened again. "Four years!"

Jason nodded.

Providencia   Deborah A. Hodge

Tom moved forward in his chair again. "How long since you've heard from her?"

"Four years."

Tom chewed on his lip, pausing to reflect on what he had just heard. "Let me see if I have this straight. You haven't seen her or heard from her since she left for Ecuador."

Jason shook his head. "No, I haven't."

Tom continued to chew on his lip and narrowed his eyes as he attempted to process what he had heard. "So things ended with you two?"

Jason nodded and pain once again took over his eyes and face. "We thought it would be better that way. We were convinced that God couldn't be leading us to be together if He was leading us to different fields of service."

Tom tried to absorb what Jason was saying as he repeated, "You both were convinced."

Jason nodded, sighed, and said, "Yeah."

"But you still have feelings for her."

Jason took a deep breath as he lowered his head. "I do. I've tried so hard not to, but I do."

Tom rubbed his forehead. "I see. That's the problem. You're afraid of struggling with the same situation again."

Jason shifted in his seat. "Yeah, I'm struggling all right, but it's not the same situation."

Tom tilted his head and narrowed his eyes. "It's not?"

Jason shook his head and let out a sigh of frustration and sadness. "No, the problem is Sarah's moved on, and I haven't."

"What do you mean she's moved on?"

"She's engaged."

"If you haven't communicated with her, how do you know?"

"Her grandfather told me."

Chapter 1

Tom frowned. "Her grandfather?"

Jason nodded. "My seminary mentor, John Jones, is Sarah's grandfather."

Tom picked up his water. "I see."

"He knew about the mission trip, knew I might run into Sarah since her parents are American missionaries, there, too, and so he told me that she's engaged to a doctor she's been dating for about eight months."

"I'm sorry."

Jason squirmed as he voiced his inner turmoil. "Tom, I just don't understand what God's doing here. For four years, I've done everything I know to surrender my feelings for Sarah to God. I want His will for my life, and I don't understand why I still have feelings for her when she obviously has none for me."

Jason could hear a brotherly tone as Tom spoke. "You don't know that for certain."

"She's engaged to another guy. I think that makes it pretty obvious."

"Didn't you give her license to when you broke up with her?" Tom asked honestly.

Jason's head jerked up and a look of hurt flashed in his eyes at Tom's question.

Tom was shocked at Jason's response. "I'm sorry. I made my deduction from what you told me, and the fact that you have not communicated with her in four years."

Jason closed his eyes and shook his head in frustration. "It's okay. I guess you're right."

"You've dated other girls since Sarah, haven't you?"

Jason winced and confessed. "Yeah sporadically, but none of them measured up to Sarah."

Tom rose from his chair, walked around and leaned on his desk. "Man, you have it bad."

Fidgeting, Jason answered. "Yeah, I do. That's why I am so confused about what God is doing. I know what Sarah and I agreed on, but I also

---

Providencia　　　　　　　　　　　　　　　　　　　*Deborah A. Hodge*

know what I feel. It's killing me to know that she's moved on and forgotten all about me. To make matters worse, it's possible I'll see her in ten days."

Tom put his hand on Jason's shoulder. "You don't know for sure that you're going to see her. Ecuador's a big place."

Jason blew out a breath. "No, but I'm scared to death that I might. I'd give anything if I could get out of going to Ecuador."

"But you can't."

"No, I can't. Since Dr. Cohen can't go, it's my responsibility."

Tom took a drink of water. "Maybe, it's a good thing you're going."

Jason's head shot up. "How?"

With his hand on Jason's shoulder again, Tom answered, "Maybe, it will give you closure concerning Sarah."

Jason took a deep breath before he spoke. "Or maybe it will be torture."

"Jas, you don't know that you will even see her."

"No, I don't, but I am scared to death that I will."

"Maybe that's why God has allowed this. Maybe he wants you to confront your fear, as well as your feelings for Sarah, whether you see her or not."

"Maybe."

"Whatever He has in mind will be for your good and His glory."

Jason nodded. "Yeah, I know. Thanks, I knew you'd say what I needed to hear."

Tom smiled. "Glad to be of service. How else can I help?"

Jason paused before he answered. His eyes narrowed, and he sighed before he summoned resoluteness. "You can pray for me."

Tom nodded. "Of course, I'll be praying for you."

"Thanks."

Chapter 7

"Thank you for sharing with me."

"Thanks for being willing to listen and for giving me a godly perspective."

Tom sat on the desk near Jason. "Want some more advice?"

"Yeah," Jason answered, meeting Tom's eyes.

"Hang in there. I know it's not easy, but God is faithful. He'll get you through this."

Jason rose to shake his hand. "Thanks, Tom."

Tom stood. "Anytime. Why don't you come over for dinner tonight? Edith's been after me for weeks to get you to come."

"Thanks, but I can't tonight. I have to meet with Rachael."

"Why don't you bring her to dinner? Edith would love that."

"I'm sure she would, and so would Rachael. They've both been trying to match-make for a long time."

Tom grinned. "That's true."

"Yeah, and I don't want to encourage her. Sorry I can't come tonight, maybe some other time. "

"Sure, but Rachael's a nice girl."

"Yeah, I know, but…"

Tom smiled. "But she's not Sarah."

Jason nodded as he looked at his watch. "No, but she's probably waiting on me so I'd better go."

On his way to meet Rachael, Jason took time to pray. "God help me. I don't want to get out of your will. Please prepare my heart for what lies ahead in Ecuador. Please make me useable and a reflection of you."

When he opened the door to his office, Rachael was waiting.

She frowned as he walked in. "I was beginning to think that you'd forgotten."

He sat down across from her. "I'm sorry. I had a meeting with Tom. It lasted a little longer than I thought."

"I've brought the preaching team assignments for your approval."

"Wow, Roy finished them."

"Yep, this afternoon." She handed the papers to him and he felt her intentionally brush his hand in the process.

Without reacting, he took the papers. "Let's take a look. Team One: Roy, Matthew, Hunter, Ryan, Catherine; Team Two: Cannon, Maisen, Shannon and Lane, and Team Three: Thomas, Cole, Anna, Payton and Brandon; Team Four: Collin, Brooke , Melissa, and Jack; Team Five: You, Kelsey, Allyson and me." Jason shot a look in Rachael's direction. "I didn't know you were going."

"Neither did I until Roy offered me the opportunity today. Ellen backed out because of family problems."

"I don't see the list of preaching stations and assignments."

"Oh, didn't I give them to you?" Looking in her case, Rachael found the papers. "I'm sorry. I thought I gave them all to you."

Chapter 2

Jason reached for the papers. "That's okay. Let's see, five churches and four missions. That's nine preaching stations and five teams for two and a half weeks. That's great. What about the translators?"

Rachael moved to where she could peer over his shoulder. "They should be there." Jason tried to ignore her proximity. She reached over his shoulder and turned the page. He shifted in his seat. Two pages were stuck together. When Rachael realized it, she reached with her other arm over his other shoulder so she could use both hands to free the pages. Jason tried to ignore how close she was and how good she smelled. His heart rate quickened and he tried to control his breathing so she would not know the effect she was having.

"There, I knew they should be there." Once she was successful in separating the pages, she retreated to her position directly behind him.

He was relieved. He exhaled a small, quiet "whew" and silently looked at the papers.

His relief was short-lived as she positioned a hand on each side of him, and leaned over his shoulder again. Once again, he could smell her hair and knew that if he turned his head slightly to the left, he would be cheek to cheek with her. He knew she was aware of his struggle when she asked, "Is everything all right?"

Again, he summoned his self-control. "Yep, everything looks good."

"I'll tell Roy that everything is good to go." She slid around to gather up the papers to put them back in her briefcase.

Jason handed her the papers. "Thanks. I'll call tomorrow and thank him personally."

"He'll appreciate that," she said, while closing her briefcase. "I'll make you copies of everything, and make sure you get them tomorrow."

"Thanks."

As she finished fastening her briefcase, she glanced up, smiled, and suggested, "I know you haven't had dinner. Would you like to grab a bite before you head home?"

Jason's mouth tightened as he heard her request. The pause was palpable.

Rachael folded her arms and shook her head with frustration. "Hey, all I am proposing is dinner."

Providencia   *Deborah A. Hodge*

Jason nodded, but remained silent.

Still with arms folded, Rachael tapped her foot.

"So does the nod mean yes or no?"

Jason raised his head and looked directly at her with narrowed eyes. She let out a long, deep sigh, and turned on her heels to go.

"Forget it. I'll see you tomorrow."

Not wanting to leave things as they were, Jason called out, "Wait, Rachael, I owe you an explanation."

She stopped and slowly turned around. Her face revealed anger and hurt. Jason eyes narrowed again as he searched for just the right words to say.

"Rachael you're a nice girl, but," Jason paused, as he saw Rachael's reaction. She folded her arms again, and the foot tapping returned. He wasn't sure whether to continue or not. Her jaw clenched and her anger was obvious. He groped for words and blurted out, "It's not you; it's me."

Rachael threw her head back and looked at the ceiling as her foot tapping quickened. "That's funny."

He heard the sarcasm, but decided to ask anyway. "What's funny?"

"The old it's me not you speech. That's what you say when it really *is* the other person, but you're trying not to hurt my feelings."

"It's not a speech. It really *is* me, and I really don't want to hurt your feelings. That's why I'm trying to be honest."

The toe tapping stopped and her posture stiffened as she turned her head and gave him a sideways glance. "So may I ask why you say it's you?"

He gave a hesitant nod, swallowed and continued. "Let's just say that I'm haunted by a ghost from the past."

Rachael sat down and probed, "A girl ghost?"

He nodded again in confirmation. "Yeah, a girl ghost."

"Is she the one that got away?"

Chapter 2

Jason nodded again as sadness overtook his face. "The one that got away."

Rachael reached out and touched his arm. "Difficult to talk about?"

"Yeah," Jason answered as he put his thumb across his jaw and covered his mouth with his hand.

"Okay, how about this? Let's be friends."

Jason shifted in his seat as he tried to get a read.

Realizing his skepticism, she added, "Friends without expectation of anything more."

His eyes widened and he dropped his hand from his mouth. "Are you sure?"

She summoned a smile that was not very convincing. "I'm sure. Now how about having dinner with a friend?"

His hand covered his mouth again, and frowned.

Rachael smiled and shook her head. She raised her right hand while crossing her heart with the other. "No expectations, I promise. Now how about dinner? I'm hungry."

Jason still wasn't sure he believed her, but he allowed his frown to turn into a sheepish grin as he reluctantly agreed to have dinner.

Rachael chose to have dinner at a very small diner close to the seminary and much to his surprise it was a very enjoyable experience. He learned more about Rachael than he ever had before. The foremost thing he learned was that she was a very nice girl and not at all the man-hungry siren he had imagined.

"Where did you grow up?"

"I grew up in Texas," she answered as she took another sip of iced tea, "and you?"

"Kansas."

"Born and raised right here, huh?"

"Yep," he answered as he wiped his mouth with his napkin.

"How about college?"

"UK."

Rachael nodded as she put down her fork to take another sip of tea. As she raised her glass, she asked, "Seminary?"

"Midwestern," he answered as he dug into his mash potatoes with his fork.

With raised eyebrows and a pat of her mouth with her napkin, Rachael responded, "Wow, Kansas all the way."

He nodded, "Except for the time I was in Iowa."

She tilted her head and pursed her mouth with interest. "Iowa," she repeated.

"Uh-huh, I was pastor of a church there for two years," Jason said as he took another bite of meatloaf.

"And then back to the seminary?"

Dabbing his mouth with his napkin while reaching for his tea, Jason answered, "Yep, how about you? How'd you get from Texas to here?"

"I attended Baylor, where I did summer missions every summer, attended Southwestern briefly, and wound up here."

"If you don't mind my asking, why did you leave Southwestern?"

Rachael shook her head. "No, I don't mind. Roy and my father are friends. Roy told my father that he needed an assistant and that a tuition break came with the job. He asked if I might be interested. I prayed about it and felt God's leadership to come here."

Jason stopped chewing. "And so you became an assistant for both of us."

Rachael put her fork down for another sip of tea. "That's right."

"So what do you expect to do after seminary?"

"Whatever God wants me to do."

Jason smiled. "And what do you think that might be?"

"I don't know. I am one of those 'who signed the blank paper.'"

Chapter 2

Jason gave her a smile of approval. "One of those willing to let God fill in the blanks."

Rachael's face lit up. "Exactly."

"And you thought Midwestern was one of the blanks?"

Rachael tilted her head, fingered the rim of her tea glass, and confessed, "I did, and then I thought you might be one of the blanks."

Trying to look surprised, he answered, "Really!"

She smiled. "I didn't know. I've been praying about it, and thought I would explore the possibility. However, you haven't been very cooperative."

"Sorry about that. I've been doing some struggling of my own."

Rachael nodded, "With ghosts."

Jason wiped his mouth. "Yeah, with ghosts and God's will."

"I'll be praying for you." Rachael said as she took a bite of mashed potatoes.

Jason smiled. "I'll pray for you too."

Rachael smiled and winked a flirty wink. "Thanks friend."

Jason's eyes narrowed and he let out a slight huff.

Rachael shook with laughter at his reaction. "Just kidding. You have to lighten up. You're way too serious."

Jason smiled. He stopped eating, sat back, and chewed on his new admiration for Rachael. He'd known her for about a year, so how had he not known these things about her? He stared at her without realizing it.

She blushed. "What?"

"Huh?"

Her face revealed her embarrassment. "You're staring."

Jason was the embarrassed one now. "I am. I'm sorry; I didn't realize that I was."

Rachael grinned at his embarrassment. "So what's up?"

Providencia   *Deborah A. Hodge*

Jason looked down. "Nothing, I just can't believe that I didn't know these things about you."

"What things?"

"All that stuff about your background," he hesitated, "and that you're so much fun."

"Wow," she gave a little laugh and continued. "Well, it could be because we've never talked about anything but work."

Jason looked up, grinned sheepishly and said, "Yeah that might be it. Sorry about that, my fault entirely."

Rachel sat up straight, cocked her head, smiled a crooked smile and replied, "It sure was."

Jason was dumbfounded. He frowned while Rachael erupted in laughter. Jason joined her. *Why did I never take the time to get to know her? She's great. If it weren't for Sarah, I probably could fall in love wi-th her.*

It was the beginning of a genuine friendship. Jason enjoyed Rachael's company, and other meals followed in the next few days. Spending time with Rachael gave him less time to think about Sarah. He was glad that Rachael would be going to Ecuador.

Chapter 2

Providencia   Deborah A. Hodge

On departure day the seminary entourage was at the airport, busily checking in and chattering like magpies as they made their way through security and toward the gate. The chatter continued as the group waited for the boarding call.

Once on the plane and in the air, everyone conversed with his or her seatmates. Jason was glad to have the good fortune of having Rachael as his.

"It's nice to see everyone so excited about the trip," Rachael said, as she flipped her hair over her shoulder and perused the airline magazine.

"Yeah, it is," Jason answered, shuffling through the lists of trip assignments and details.

"Something wrong?"

"Roy informed me at the airport that Katty had called and said that one of the translators backed out today."

"So what do we do?"

"Katty's looking for a replacement, and we pray that she finds one."

"We have nine. Can't we make it with nine?"

"Maybe with the preaching, we have at least five translators with adequate skills to translate for preaching, but we'll need more for door-to-door evangelism."

"I see. So we'll pray that Katty is successful."

Turning his attention back to the papers, Jason said, "I'll try to come up with a contingency plan in case she isn't."

Chapter 3

"Oh ye of little faith."

Looking up from the papers, Jason responded, "No, just a leader who must be prepared."

Rachael smiled. "Gotcha. I'll get back to my magazine and leave you alone."

By the time the plane arrived in Houston, Jason had a contingency plan. Roy looked it over and agreed. "I hope Katty finds another translator, but if she doesn't we'll go with your plan."

"I hope she does. It would be a shame to not be able to take advantage of every evangelizing opportunity we have

"It surely would," Roy said as he handed the plan to Jason. "Would either of you be interested in grabbing a bite? We have a little over two hours before we get on the plane."

Jason looked at Rachael. "Sounds good."

Rachael agreed, "Let's go."

Rachael walked between both of her bosses as they headed toward a nearby restaurant. The meal and conservation lasted until fifteen minutes before boarding. Realizing it was almost time to board, Roy paid the check and the trio headed to their gate just in time to hear the boarding call.

Once again, Rachael was Jason's seatmate.

Rachael laughed. "I guess we are fated to be together."

Jason gave her a stern side glance.

With raised eyebrows, Rachel observed, "Wow, I haven't seen that look in a while."

"I haven't heard a statement like that in a while."

She cocked her head and gave him a look. "I was talking about the seating, doofus, don't be so paranoid."

"Sorry, I'm just a little stressed."

She frowned and said, "I thought we had moved past all this."

Providencia   *Deborah A. Hodge*

Jason took a deep breath and let it out. "We have. I'm sorry."

The pilot interrupted their conversation with announcements, after which Rachael pulled out a book and began reading. Jason closed his eyes and tried to relax. In four and a half hours, they would land in Ecuador. The specter of Sarah loomed large in his thoughts. His mind replayed the full-length version of the last time they were together.

"I know you have accepted the call to the little church in Iowa, but is there any way you might be wrong about God's leading?"

Jason knew his face betrayed his concern at the foreboding her question suggested. He stood erect and silent for a moment as he scanned her face for clues. The deep sadness he discovered in Sarah's eyes became contagious and caused his heart to hurt. He shifted and shook his head. "No, I told you. I am sure this is God's will for me."

Tears puddled in her eyes and glistened as they ran down her face. "I don't know what to do."

Jason pulled her into his arms. She buried her face in his chest and sobbed. He hugged her tighter. "We both know what to do. We just don't like it."

She nodded and sobbed some more. He didn't say anything. He just held her and stroked her hair as she cried. Finally, she spoke. "Could we really have been that wrong about us?"

He choked back tears as he answered, "I don't know anymore."

Sarah back away. "What do you mean by that?"

"I mean I thought we were doing God's will, but the way things have worked out I don't know anymore."

Tears flowing freely again, Sarah pleaded, "Don't you love me anymore?"

Stunned that she would ask, Jason took her by the shoulders. "Of course I do. I love you with all my heart, but sometimes that's not enough."

Sarah stared at him in disbelief. "What's that supposed to mean?"

"Sarah, you and I both know that being in the center of God's will is the most important thing in life."

Chapter 3

She nodded slowly, tears streaming again.

Jason continued haltingly, "We have prayed sincerely about how He wants us to serve Him, with me it's the church in Iowa, with you it's the hospital in Ecuador. I wish it weren't so, but we both know it is."

"But what does that say about us?"

"I don't know."

"You asked me to marry you and I accepted. We both believed it was God's will."

"I know."

"But now you're not sure."

"I'm not sure about anything anymore except that God wants me at the church in Iowa. Are you sure He wants you in Ecuador?"

"I think so."

"You think so? I thought you were sure."

"When I pray about it I am sure. When I'm with you, I'm not so sure."

"I know what you mean. When I am with you, it's all I can do to keep from rebelling against Iowa."

"I know," Sarah said, as she fell into his arms.

"Sarah I cannot put you and my feelings for you above God, and neither can you. We must put Him first and be totally surrendered."

"But how do we do that?"

"The same way Abraham was willing to sacrifice Isaac. Because Abraham was willing to sacrifice Isaac on the altar, God knew that He had the preeminent place in Abraham's heart and life. We have to be willing to do that too, you with me and me with you."

"You're willing to give me up."

"I'm willing to give you to the Lord."

"But, what if He doesn't give me back to you like He did with Isaac and Abraham?"

"I think God wants *me* to give you to Him and *you* to give me to Him with no assurance that He will give us back to each other."

"How do we do that?"

"By God's grace and strength."

"I don't know if I can."

"I know, but we have to."

"But, we can stay in touch, right?"

"I don't think so."

The shock on Sarah's face was apparent as she pushed away from him.

"So, you're breaking up with me."

"I'm giving you to the Lord."

"You're cutting us off from one another."

"I believe that's really the only way we can give each other totally into the Lord's hands."

"So you're breaking the engagement."

"For now."

"What's that supposed to mean?"

"Sarah I cannot give you to the Lord and stay in touch constantly hoping that God will change His mind and send me to Ecuador or you to Iowa."

"Why not?"

"That's not total surrender. I don't think it works that way. I think it must be all or nothing."

"All or nothing," Sarah echoed in disbelief.

"I'm sorry. I think it has to be that way."

Sarah backed away, turned away, folded her arms, and shook her head to gain clarity.

Chapter 3

"So this is it. We just call the whole thing off. I go my way and you go your way."

"I guess, but we're doing it because we are surrendering each other to God."

"You really think that we are a mistake, don't you?"

"It's not that. I'm just trying to do what I think God is asking us to do."

"Maybe God's just asking us to wait about getting married."

"Maybe, but how do we do that if you're in Ecuador and I'm in Iowa?"

"I don't know, but if God wants us together He can bring us together."

"I know He can. That's why I am trying to put us in His hands."

"So you really are hoping He will."

"Of course, but I have to give Him that hope, too, and so do you. We have to surrender it all to Him."

"I know you're right. I just don't think I can handle losing you."

"Maybe you won't lose me."

"Only God knows."

"Only God knows, and we can trust Him."

"I know. I'm just scared."

"Me too, but I know we can trust Him. He knows what He's doing."

"So you go to Iowa, I go to Ecuador, and we leave us in His hands. We don't keep in touch. We leave us in His hands."

"So you do understand what I'm saying?"

"I do. I don't like it, but I do understand."

He held out his hand. "I don't like it either, but why don't we pray about it?"

Providencia   Deborah A. Hodge

Sarah took his hand and they knelt and prayed. Jason began, "Lord here we are trying to be faithful and obedient to You. We don't understand why You led us together only to lead us apart, but we are willing to commit each other to You and surrender our lives into Your hands.

Father it's the hardest thing You've ever asked us to do. Please help us to do it. In Jesus' name I pray."

Sarah squeezed his hand as she prayed. "Lord, You know how hard this is, and You know we want You to be first in our lives. You have to help me. I cannot do this in my own strength."

"Please Lord, I don't understand, but I am willing to trust You. As much as I can, I am surrendering us to you. I want to want what You want. Please help me." She paused to wipe tears and clear her nose. Jason squeezed her hand. Her voice cracked as she continued. "I want to put it all in Your hands and let you take care of the future. I give Jason to You, even if that means we're ... never together again. In Jesus' name I pray. Amen."

As Sarah opened her eyes, she saw that Jason was crying too. She put her other arm around him and he responded by hugging her with tender strength. They stood up with arms holding each other.

Jason stifled his tears, swallowed hard and said, "This is so hard."

Sarah nodded, tears streaming again. She licked the tears from her lips as she wiped tears from her eyes. "But we have to. I know you're right. God brought us together the first time. Maybe He'll do it again."

They both knew they had to say goodbye, but it didn't come easily. They held each other for a while longer and finally faced the kiss goodbye.

Chapter 3

Providencia   *Deborah A. Hodge*

The past gave way to the present as Jason heard Rachael calling his name.

"Jay, are you okay?"

"Huh?"

"Are you okay?"

"Yeah, why?"

"I think you were having a bad dream. Your face was contorted; you were mumbling something in your sleep."

Embarrassed by the episode, Jason apologized. "I'm sorry. I didn't realize I was asleep ... I didn't mean to go to sleep. I am sorry if I disturbed you."

"I wasn't asleep. You are very stressed, aren't you?"

Jason rubbed his face, wondering what Rachael had heard him say. "Yeah."

"Would you like to talk about it?"

Jason shook his head. "No, I don't think."

Rachael patted his arm. "Come on, it might help."

He decided to test what she had heard. "Did I say anything that I shouldn't have?"

"I couldn't really understand what you were mumbling. I just wondered if it had something to do with your ghost."

Chapter 4

Her statement caused Jason to shoot a telltale glance in Rachael's direction.

Rachael put her arm around his "Sorry I wish I could make the ghost disappear."

Putting his hand on hers, Jason admitted, "You help more than you know."

Rachael smiled. "That's what friends are for."

Jason returned her smile. "Thanks."

She handed him a piece of paper. "The flight attendant passed out these forms to fill out and turn in as we enter the country. We touch down in about twenty minutes."

"Thanks again."

The silence between them was palpable as he filled out the forms.

"Ecuador at last, aren't you excited?" Rachael asked as she peered out the window.

As the plane touched down, turmoil intruded on Jason's composure. He was the professor in charge and yet he was not in charge of his own emotions.

Noticeably unenthusiastic, Jason answered, "Yeah."

Rachael gave him a quick once-over. "Something wrong?"

Unconvincingly, Jason replied, "Nope."

He could tell by Rachael's face that she was confused, but he hoped she would let it go. He got his wish, but he knew she was watching him as he retrieved their belongings from the overhead and made conversation with others in the group. He knew she knew something was wrong.

Making their way through customs, the group continued to the baggage claim and screening. Because he knew Katty Gándara, Roy led the group from there. As they made their way to the entrance of the airport, Roy spied Katty waving.

"Buenas noches," Katty greeted enthusiastically.

Providencia   *Deborah A. Hodge*

"Hello, how are you?" Roy asked.

"I am well. How are you?"

Pointing to Jason, Roy continued, "Katty, may I introduce Jason Parks? Jason, this is Katty Gándara."

Katty stuck out her hand. "Pleased to meet you Mr. Jason."

"It's just Jason. Please call me Jason. I am very pleased to finally meet you."

Katty smiled broadly. "How is Professor Cohen?"

"He is doing much better since his surgery," Jason answered.

Katty's eyes brightened at the news. "That is very good news. I have been praying for him."

"Thank you. He will be very glad to hear that."

Katty motioned toward the front entrance. "Everyone is waiting to meet all of you."

Jason smiled. "Great!"

"Oh, and I have found another translator."

"That's fantastic Katty," Roy said.

"Yeah it is. She's an American who is fluent in Spanish. Rodrigo says she's great."

"American, huh?"

Katty nodded. Jason held his breath as his fears ran wild.

As they made their way toward where the translators were gathered to greet them, Jason's fears proved to be on target. Among the other translators, he recognized Sarah's silhouette. *God help me. It is Sarah.* Without realizing it, he stopped dead in his tracks.

Concerned, Rachael gently touched his arm. "Something wrong?"

Realizing he had stopped, he shook his head and willed himself forward.

Seeing his ashen face, Rachael tried again. "Are you all right?"

Chapter 4

He nodded and forced an answer, "Uh-huh."

Katty interrupted the chain of events as she got the attention of the translators. "Everyone, this is Jason Parks and Roy White, the leaders of the mission team."

Jason responded without looking directly at Sarah. Roy quickly introduced the rest of the team. Katty reciprocated by introducing the translators. Jason gave his full attention and smiled as Katty introduced each one until she came to Sarah. Jason responded to her introduction without looking directly at her. No one noticed the difference except Sarah and Rachael.

Katty motioned, "Okay, the buses are over here."

———•———

The group moved to the buses and the girls filed on board as the guys, along with the bus drivers, busily loaded the luggage. Determined to investigate her observations, Rachael made sure that she boarded the same bus as Sarah. She made her way down the aisle and sat by Sarah.

"Hi," she chirped. "I'm Rachael. May I sit with you?"

"Of course. I'm Sarah," Sarah answered, scooting over to make sure Rachael had room.

Wrestling her pack from her back, Rachael fell into the seat with a sigh.

"Tired?" Sarah asked with a smile.

"Very, but it's been a great trip so far."

"I hope it will continue to be."

Rachael probed, "You're an American, aren't you?"

"Yes, but I've lived most of my life in Ecuador."

"Really."

"My parents are missionaries here," Sarah added as she glanced out the window.

"I see," Rachael said, tracing the object of Sarah's pensive glance.

Rachael was not surprised to see Jason outside the window. It was

Providencia   Deborah A. Hodge

clear that these two not only knew each other but had a history. *Maybe she's why I can't get anywhere with Jason. If so, Sarah was an exquisitely beautiful ghost. Her long, light brown hair, big brown eyes, dark complexion and tall, slender body accentuated her beauty.* Rachael clenched her teeth. *I am so jealous.*

Someone calling Sarah's name interrupted Rachael's reflections. Rachael watched as a very attractive Ecuadorian man walked toward their seat. Still focused on Jason, Sarah was oblivious to his voice or approach.

"Sarah, do you not hear me?"

Jarred from her thoughts, Sarah was surprised to see him. "Christian!"

"Yes, could I talk with you for a moment?"

"Of course."

"Could we step outside?"

"Sure," Sarah answered as Rachael stood for her to exit. As Sarah made her way to the aisle, Christian gently took her arm and helped her. He then stepped back to allow Sarah to go first. It was apparent that there was something more than friendship between Sarah and him.

As they stepped from the bus, Rachael turned her attention to Jason. He was standing with Roy and Katty but his attention was riveted on Sarah and Christian. Christian shot a glance toward Jason. Jason looked away. Sarah's head turned toward Jason, too. Christian's face was not a happy one. Sarah said something and Christian responded. Rachael watched with great interest as the conversation continued and ended with Christian hugging Sarah goodbye. *Um-hum, the drama thickens. I believe we have a triangle. From Jason's reaction when he saw her, Sarah must be his ghost. Maybe Christian is the ghost-buster and I will have a chance with Jason after all.*

Chapter 4

Providencia   *Deborah A. Hodge*

Trying not to be obvious, Jason watched too. After the goodbye, Sarah boarded the bus, and Christian got in his car and drove away. Jason watched Sarah board the bus and walk toward her seat with Rachael. Once Sarah returned to her seat, Jason returned to his conversation with Roy and Katty but kept an eye toward the bus. He wondered whether Rachael had figured out that Sarah was his ghost.

Jason noticed that when Katty boarded the bus, Sarah excused herself and moved to sit with Katty. Shortly after, Jason boarded the bus and purposefully avoided looking in Sarah's direction as he made his way to sit with Rachael. Though he was sitting with Rachael, he was watching Katty and her seatmate.

"Is everything all right?"

Jason's eyes narrowed and his jaw tightened as he answered, "Everything's fine."

Rachael touched his arm. "Are you sure?"

"I'm sure." His face told a different story.

Rachael gripped his arm, "You know Sarah. Don't you?"

His eyes flashed, and his voice betrayed a tinge of anger. "I used to."

"I think she was more than an acquaintance."

His mouth tightened as he answered hesitantly. "Once upon a time."

"Is she the ghost, the one that got away?"

He didn't answer. Rachael craned her neck and looked directly at him as she squeezed his arm again.

Chapter 5

"She is, isn't she? She's the ghost girl."

Without looking directly at her, Jason frowned and answered abruptly. "Look I have a lot on my mind. We can play twenty questions later."

Rachael withdrew her hand, folded her arms and turned toward the window. "You don't have to bite my head off."

Jason closed his eyes, shook his head and let out a sigh. "I'm sorry. I didn't mean to. I'm just tired."

"Okay," Rachael said, "but I know I'm right. Sarah's the ghost girl."

Jason did not respond. He laid his head back and rested. He hoped that Rachael would let it drop. He didn't want her to know that she was right, and he didn't want to face what he was feeling. *God help me! Now that I am here and face-to-face with Sarah, I can't handle it. Help me please! I don't know what to do. Please help me not to make a fool of myself. Help me to trust you and to leave it in Your hands.*

The bus ride from the airport to the Nazarene Seminary where they would be staying was approximately thirty minutes. Jason continued to pray with his eyes closed and head back. He could feel Rachael watching. He didn't know if she was truly trying to be a friend or was just nosey or jealous. Regardless of which one it was, he couldn't handle any one of those scenarios right now. His only hope was that God would come to his rescue.

Arrival at the seminary brought some relief. Roy barked out the room assignments as the rest of the men unloaded luggage and carried it to the rooms. Jason made sure he put distance between himself and Sarah and Rachael. He was tired physically, mentally and emotionally. Surely a night's sleep would help.

Roy had made room assignments back in Kansas. There were two missionaries and two translators in some rooms. It turned out that Rachael and Sarah shared the same room. Surely during the eighteen days of the trip Rachael would have time to wheedle the truth out of Sarah.

After helping unpack the bus and making sure the luggage went to the right rooms, Jason found his way to a deserted place on the seminary grounds and poured his heart out to God.

"God help me here. I don't understand what You're trying to do. Father, she's as beautiful as ever, but she's totally unavailable. If I had any doubts, seeing her and her fiancé together tonight dispelled them. What do I do God? I know that I still love her. There's no doubt about it. Please

Providencia   *Deborah A. Hodge*

help me not to give in to these feelings. Please help me be able to do my job while I'm here and to let Sarah go into Your hands."

Just as he was finishing his prayer, he heard someone walking up the steps from where the rooms were located. The moonlight silhouetted the person. Jason let out a whisper. "Oh God, it's Sarah. Please don't let her come this way. I can't do a one-on-one, not now." He melted back into the shadows as he watched her proceed across the seminary grounds opposite from where he was. He realized that she was praying also. He wondered if she could possibly be talking to God about him. He wanted to sneak over and see, but knew that it would be an invasion of privacy. Even though he decided to give her space, there was no way for him to go to his room without her seeing him. He had no choice but to wait for her to go back to her room. He had to stay where he was, and that presented him with the temptation to watch her from a distance.

The sight of Sarah walking in the moonlight ignited a complete spectrum of feelings. He found himself crying out to God again. "God please help me. I feel deep sadness and regret at saying goodbye four years ago. I feel strong love for Sarah, longing to be with her, and shame and guilt over having these feeling for an engaged woman. Please deliver me from all of these feelings and please let Sarah go to her room."

God graciously answered his prayer. He watched Sarah walk toward the steps that led to her room. "Thank you Father." He quietly and slowly followed. As he reached the steps, he listened for her footfall. Not hearing any, he proceeded to his room.

Roy was still awake. "Jay are you all right?"

"I'm okay."

He rose up from his bunk and positioned himself on his elbow. "Are you sure? You're not acting quite like yourself."

Jason sat down on his own bunk. "I'm just a little stressed."

"Would you like to talk? I'm a good listener. It might help."

Jason stretched out on the bunk. "Thanks buddy, but this is something God and I have to work out."

"Okay, I'll be praying for you."

"Thanks Roy. I need it."

Chapter 5

Providencia   *Deborah A. Hodge*

Rachael's concerted effort to learn the truth began the next day at breakfast. Her barrage began with a volley of implications to test Sarah's response. She soon found that Sarah was as unwilling to admit to anything as Jason was.

"Sarah you told me last night that your parents were missionaries here. What do you do?"

"I'm a nurse at a mission hospital," Sarah answered as she took a bite of toast.

Swallowing a sip of coffee, Rachael unleashed the next volley. "I'll bet that's exciting. I'm a secretary at the seminary."

Sarah wiped her mouth with her napkin. "My work can be exciting. I'm sure your work at the seminary is rewarding too."

"Yeah, Roy and Jason are great." Sarah stopped chewing, swallowed hard, and wiped her mouth again.

"You work for Roy and … Jason."

"I do." Rachael could tell by Sarah's tone that she had hit her mark. She took another shot. "I got the impression last night that you and Jason know each other."

Without looking at Rachael directly, Sarah poked her food with her fork. "Yeah, I knew Jason when I was studying nursing at the University of Kansas."

"He's a great guy, isn't he?"

That shot caused a pensiveness to return to Sarah's face. She didn't answer immediately.

Chapter 6

Rachael decided to repeat the question. "He's a great guy, isn't he?"

The repeating of the question jarred a reluctant response. Sarah stopped poking her food, and without looking up, she answered, "Yes, he is."

As if on cue, Jason entered the dining hall.

Waving to Jason, Rachael announced, "Look, there he is now. Maybe, he'll sit with us."

Sarah's head shot up, and as she spied Jason, she said, "If you'll excuse me, I need to take care of something before we leave."

As Sarah quickly gathered her tray and hurried away, Rachael replied, "Sure, I'll see you later."

Pleased with her first attempt at extracting information, Rachael relished the moment. *Wow! She overreacts just as much as he does. Something tells me that the history isn't really history. Where does that leave me?*

After breakfast the leaders called a meeting for a brief devotional time, as well as introductions and assignments. When time for introduction of the interpreters to the rest of the team members and assignments came, Rachael was chagrined to find that assignments had been adjusted and she and Sarah would be part of Roy's team and not Jason's. Jason's interpreter was Luz Gutierrez. That meant that although they would be canvassing in the same area, Rachael would not be able to observe Sarah-Jason interactions, but maybe she could probe Sarah again and find out more.

Once Roy had made the assignments and given instructions, the teams boarded the buses and headed for the mission church sponsored by Bible Baptist Church. The mission was on the outskirts of Quito and quite a distance from the seminary. Sarah sat with Roy and Rachael sat with Katty at the front of the bus. While Roy and Sarah conversed about what lay ahead, Rachael quietly made inquiries about Sarah.

"Good morning, Katty. I'm Rachael Davis, the one with whom you have spoken whenever you called the office. It's nice to finally meet you."

"It is very nice to meet you, Rachael. Is this your first trip to Ecuador?

Rachael nodded. "Yes."

"How do you like my country?"

"It is very beautiful. I especially like the mountains." Rachael waved toward the mountains that surrounded the city.

"Yes, they are beautiful. They are volcanoes, you know."

Rachael's eyes popped and a twinge of concern captured her face. "No, I didn't know."

Katty smiled. "There isn't any danger. They are not very active just now."

Rachael breathed a sigh of relief. "That's good."

Katty nodded. "What do you do at the seminary besides answer the phone?"

"I am Roy and Jason's secretary, as well as a student."

"I see. Roy seems very nice and so does Jason."

Rachael smiled and nodded. "They are. Tell me about yourself and your business."

"I love Jesus and I love to tell others about Him. My business is to set up mission trips for various groups."

Rachael nodded toward one of the interpreters across the aisle. "How do you find all of the interpreters for the trips?"

"Some I have known for a long time. Some are recommended by people I know, and some I have worked with on other trips."

"Which category does Sarah Barnes fit?"

"She was recommended to me by my friend Rodrigo."

"So, you don't know her personally."

Katty shook her head. "No, not really, but I have known of her parents for years."

"Her parents."

"Her parents have served in Ecuador as missionaries for years."

"Sarah told me that she was a nurse at a mission hospital."

"Yes, she told me also. She is a nurse at the hospital in Otavalo, and I

Chapter 6

hear she is a very good one."

"Isn't it unusual for a nurse to serve as an interpreter?"

"Not really, some interpreters work at other jobs. They work as interpreters to earn extra money."

"Is that what Sarah is doing?"

"She is helping out because Rodrigo asked her to. When the other interpreter could not come, I could not find another in so short a time. Rodrigo asked Sarah and she agreed."

"I see. Did you know that she and Jason know each other?"

"Yes, Sarah told me."

"Do you know how they are acquainted?"

"I believe they attended university together."

The driver of the bus interrupted. He and the other driver were confused about the location of the mission site, so he asked Katty for directions. As Katty excused herself to answer his questions, Rachael was sure that she had reached a dead end concerning Katty's knowledge of Jason and Sarah's relationship.

Once the driver's quandary about the directions had been resolved, the remainder of the journey to the mission area was easy. The mission group unloaded from the two buses to meet members of Bible Baptist Church who were there to join them in the house-to-house evangelism efforts.

"Hola," Katty called to Pastor Hector.

"Hola, me hermana," Pastor Hector answered, greeting her with the customary kiss on the cheek.

"Pastor, may I introduce you to Dr. Roy White and Dr. Jason Parks?"

Each of the men thrust forward their hands and greeted one another with a handshake as they introduced the other members of their respective groups.

After the introductions Roy, Jason and Pastor Hector paired the church members with seminary teams. Once Roy read the assignments and gave instructions as well as a time to return to the buses, Jason led

---

Providencia   *Deborah A. Hodge*

the entire group in prayer, after which the groups embarked in all directions.

Rachael let out a "whew." "Wow I didn't realize the terrain would be this rugged."

Rita, a church member, smiled. "This part of Quito is uphill and downhill."

Sarah smiled and nodded. "And walkways are a narrow mixture of dirt, sand and gravel."

Rachael pointed. "And I see intermittent tall grass and trees."

Roy stopped and commented, "The treading is hard, but the fruits of labor are worth it."

"How many people live in this area?" Rachael asked Rita.

"There are many people here. Their homes are scattered along the hillsides," Rita answered. She also pointed the team's attention ahead. "Once we reach the top of that hill, we will see many working to clear land or planting furrowed fields."

"Will they be willing to stop work and speak to us?" Rachael asked.

"Sí," Rita nodded.

Rita was right; the people were willing to talk to the team and many were open to the gospel and accepted Christ as their Savior. The team took turns witnessing to people and praying while the witnessing occurred. When it was Rachael's turn, Sarah worked seamlessly with her. There was absolutely no doubt that Sarah was genuine in her love for Jesus and the people with whom Roy was sharing the gospel. There was tenderness and kindness in her voice and eyes as she turned Roy's English into Spanish. The people to whom they were witnessing responded to her as genuinely as she approached them. Rachael could see why Jason would be interested in a woman like this for reasons well beyond her beauty.

After a while, Rachael felt compelled to comment. "Sarah, I am blown away by how fantastic you are with the people."

Sarah blushed. "These people are also my people. Though I am American, I have spent most of my life in Ecuador."

"It's very obvious that you love them very much," Roy added.

"Yes I do."

"Go out into the highways and hedges and compel them to come in is what the Bible says, and your compelling is with the tenderness of the Great Shepherd," observed Gabriella, a member of Bible Baptist Church assigned to the group.

Sarah smiled and responded, "I am simply relaying Roy's words."

"Maybe," Roy said, "but you're doing it in your own unique way."

"That's a good thing," Matt joked. "Roy can be a little gruff at times."

Sarah, Rachael and the others laughed.

Roy cocked his head playfully and responded to Matt's comment. "That's Professor White to you, and you need to remember that I'm the one who has to give your final grade."

Laughing, Matt chose to kowtow. He bowed in playful homage. "Sorry, esteemed professor."

"That's better," Roy said, as everyone laughed.

Returning to the original conversation and looking directly at Sarah, Roy motioned toward everyone else. "They're right you know. You are a remarkable interpreter and witness. Thanks for letting God use you."

"You are welcome, and it is my privilege to be used."

Looking at his watch and realizing how far they had walked, Roy said, "We'd better start back toward the buses. It's almost lunch time."

Walking back, the group engaged in chitchat. Rachael soaked it all in, especially the conversation between Roy and Sarah. She moved to Sarah's side and walked lock step with Roy and her so she wouldn't miss a single word.

"I understand that you're a nurse at a mission hospital in Otavalo," Roy said to Sarah.

"Yes, I am."

"How'd you get hooked up with us?"

Even though Matt was chirping like a magpie, Rachael tried to drown

Providencia   *Deborah A. Hodge*

him out so she could hear Sarah's answer. Unsuccessful, she quickened her pace to position herself behind Roy and Sarah.

"My friend Rodrigo knows Katty. She had called him to see if he could interpret. He couldn't but said that he would see if I could. He called me and I said that I would."

"How'd you get time off from the hospital?"

"My fiancé, Christian Romero, is the doctor in charge of the hospital."

"I see. Is that the fellow you were with at the airport?"

"Yes."

"Lucky for us he said you could translate for our group."

Sarah smiled. "Lucky for me too, it's been nice getting to know you."

"You were already acquainted with Jason, weren't you?"

Rachael's ears perked up as she strained to hear the tone and words of Sarah's answer.

Sarah paused momentarily before she nodded. "I went to nursing school at the University of Kansas. I met Jason while I was there."

"Jason's a pretty good guy," Roy said. Rachael poised herself again to catch every intonation.

Sarah nodded as she gave a measured response. "Yes, he is."

Roy smiled, and added. "You're pretty great yourself."

Sarah smiled broadly. "Thanks."

Rachael chewed on what she had heard. *I was right. There was a relationship.*

Chapter 6

Providencia   *Deborah A. Hodge*

R oy's team was the last one back. Everyone else was already eating sack lunches prepared by the seminary cafeteria staff.

"We were beginning to wonder about you all," Jason said, as he handed Roy a lunch. Roy handed if off to Matt, who in turn offered it to Gabriella. Receiving another from Jason, Roy handed it to Sarah, who passed it off to Rachael.

"Here you go," Roy said. "Keep this one for yourself."

Sarah protested. "But Matt doesn't have one. He gave his to Gabriella." She handed the lunch to Matt.

Matt protested, "I'm fine, you keep it."

"I'm not very hungry. Take it, please."

Jason rose up from rummaging through the boxes of lunches. Jason looked directly at Sarah as he spoke as he thrust a bag forward. "There's plenty. The cafeteria staff provided a few extras."

Sarah stopped her protest. "Okay," Sarah said. Her eyes met Jason's as she moved forward to accept the bag. Briefly making eye contact, he handed her the lunch. "Here you go."

After a moment of eye contact and silence, Sarah managed to say, "Thanks."

"No problem," was Jason's response. He bent down again to retrieve a lunch for Roy and himself.

Sarah was slightly unnerved and greatly relieved by his cordial response. *Maybe we can be friends.*

Chapter 7

She decided to test her theory. She retrieved a drink from the ice chest, "Thanks again."

"No problem," Jason repeated without looking up. This time there was no cordiality.

Sarah frowned. *Maybe I was wrong.*

She made her way to sit with Katty and the other translators. After greetings, Sarah began to eat and they returned to their conversation about the morning's events and the week ahead. Sarah tried to listen, but her mind was elsewhere. She was watching Jason eat his lunch and replaying the events in Kansas four years before.

She could feel him as he stood holding her hands and shaking his head. "Sarah I don't get it."

Sarah looked down. "Neither do I."

Jason held tightly to her hands. "Why would God do this to us? It makes no sense that He would bring us together only to separate us."

She struggled to hold back the tears. "I don't know."

"Do you think we made a mistake?"

Sarah slipped her right hand out of his grasp and turned away. "Are you asking do I think we made a mistake in thinking we should be together or are making a mistake now?"

Jason winced. "Yes, which one do you think?"

Still turned away and with her head lowered, Sarah answered, "I've tried repeatedly to figure it out. I've gone without sleep, cried, prayed and I still don't know. All I know is God is calling me back to Ecuador and you to Iowa."

He raised her head and brushed the tears away. "Look I know it's all confusing. I think God may be testing us."

"Testing us how?"

"Testing us as he tested Abraham with Isaac to see if He really is first in our lives."

Sarah bit her lip, closed her eyes and breathed deeply. Jason was empathetic with the deep sadness and turmoil that were apparent in his body language. He pulled her close to comfort her. She surrendered briefly before she abruptly stepped back. He tried to corral her in his arms again, but she took another step back.

"Jason, God *is* first in my life."

"I know," he said.

Tears streamed from her eyes again. Hurt and sadness contorted her face. She dropped her head and confessed in a whisper, "but I also love you."

Jason stood with folded arms, sighed and pleaded, "I love you, too. So what do we do?"

After crying for a moment, Sarah looked up. "Jason, who's number one in your life?"

Jason frowned in sadness and uttered the answer they both knew. "God."

Sarah nodded. "It has to be that way for both of us. God knows our hearts."

Jason nodded. "So we put it all in God's hands. We accept the fact that God as led us away from each other. I go to Iowa and you go to Ecuador."

Sarah took a moment to summon the courage to repeat the words, "We put it in God's hands. You go to Iowa and I go to Ecuador."

"Whatever He does with our relationship is up to Him."

Sarah sighed deeply as tears streamed from her eyes, and her voice cracked as she reluctantly agreed. "We put us in God's hands and accept whatever He does."

Jason's eyes narrowed. "No long-distance relationship; I think hanging on would not be full surrender."

Sarah chewed on her lip and looked down trying to maintain control of her emotions. "So what you're saying is we're breaking up."

She watched Jason tremble as he nodded and said, "I guess so."

Sarah swallowed tears and asked in a low, tortured tone, "What if we never see each other again?"

Chapter 7

Jason answered without looking at her, "That's in God's hands."

Sarah felt as if a bad dream was engulfing her. She reached out for his arm. "Jason."

Still turned away, he sighed and said, "You know I'm right. We've got to trust God with us."

Sarah pulled at his arm. "I know we have to trust God, but I'm not convinced that means we need to break up."

Jason slowly turned to look her in the eyes. "If I am your Isaac and you're mine, we have to give each other to God and let Him do what He will."

Sarah stood with an open mouth and stared at him. "You're saying that you could come between me and God, and I could come between you and God."

Sarah nodded and let out a long, deep breath. "I understand what you're saying and even think you might be right. But I don't know how to do it. How do I just let you go, possibly never to see you again, never to hold you, I ..."

Jason begged, "Sarah this is all or nothing. If He's first, He's first. We have to put it in His hands. We can't hold back."

"I know, but..."

Jason interrupted, "No buts, that's the way it is, and you know it."

Sarah surrendered. "Yeah, I do. You're right."

"So we agree we'll put it all in His hands."

Sarah nodded. "We'll put it all in His hands."

Jason took her hand in his and put his other hand under her chin and tenderly forced her to look at him as he repeated, "We put it all in His hands. Let's pray and give it to Him." Jason voiced their prayer of total surrender and Sarah echoed her agreement with "amen." As the prayer ended, they fell into each other's arms and cried for a long time.

Once the crying had ended, they looked at each other and faced the goodbye kiss. After the kiss, she looked away and down as she summoned the courage to say what she must. Jason squeezed her hand. As she looked up, sadness flooded her face. She quickly looked away.

Providencia   *Deborah A. Hodge*

"Goodbye Jason. Take care of yourself."

Jason swallowed hard. "Bye Sarah." She nodded and turned to walk away.

Suddenly, Sarah stopped, turned and with tears streaming spoke the death knell to their relationship, "If we're going to do this thing, please don't try to call me or see me. I can't go through this again. Like you say, we'll let it all go into His hands and let Him do with us what He will."

Sarah sobbed uncontrollably all the way home and sought the comfort of her grandparents. Her grandfather was a minister and Jason's mentor and counselor. He and Mama Carrie had been there for Sarah throughout the ordeal. Neither had been surprised at the couple's final decision.

When the time came, Sarah left for Ecuador and Jason moved to Iowa.

Providencia   *Deborah A. Hodge*

Once Sarah reached Ecuador, her parents, David and Cate, became her comforters. She had kept them apprised of the situation. They were saddened by Sarah's distress but proud that she had chosen to put her relationship with Jason and her life in God's hands.

Her work at the mission hospital, prayer, and time had helped to lessen the hurt. God had been faithful to give her the strength to endure and continue to put it all in His hands. Almost immediately upon her arrival at the hospital, Dr. Christian Romero, with whom she worked, had taken an interest in her. She had not reciprocated. However, as three years passed, she having not heard from Jason and God giving her no indication that anything had changed, she opened her heart to his interest. After almost a year's courtship, she agreed to marry him.

Ironically, after a week of engagement, she had received a letter from Papa John telling her that Jason would be coming to Ecuador with a mission group from Midwestern Seminary.

"Oh, God," was her first reaction. Her parents advised her to tell Christian about Jason.

She decided to take him aside at the hospital and tell him. Sarah's body language evidenced how conflicted she was.

Christian was quite concerned. He took her hand and tenderly asked, "Sarah, what's wrong?"

"Christian there's something I need to tell you."

He held her hand tightly. "Yes, my darling."

Sarah sighed deeply and spoke slowly. "I was engaged once before."

Christian frowned. "You were. You never told me."

Chapter 8

Sarah took a deep breath and continued, "I was. He is a minister and he and I felt God was leading us into different places of service, so we called off the engagement."

Christian's eyes narrowed as he plaintively considered what she had said. After a moment, he asked, "Did you love him very much?"

Sarah knew she had to answer carefully, but honestly. Her face took on a pained expression and she bit her lip, as she answered, "I did."

"And you love me?"

"I do. You have been very good to me," she paused, "and for me."

"Do you love me like you loved him?"

Sarah paused once again. She knew Christian deserved the truth. She sighed as she answered, "I ... I don't know."

"You don't know," Christian echoed, with a tone of hurt in his voice.

Sarah dropped her head and stared at the floor. "I don't. I'm sorry if that hurts you, I don't mean to hurt you. It's just that after Jason I closed off a part of my heart. I didn't want to be hurt again like that."

Christian put his hand underneath her chin and made her look at him. "Don't you know that I'd never hurt you?"

"I know," Sarah said.

Christian brushed her hair from her eyes. "So why are you telling me about Jason now?"

Sarah sighed and bit her lip. "He's coming to Ecuador."

"I see. Is he coming to see you?"

"No, he's coming on a mission trip."

"Where?"

"Quito."

"Are you going to see him?"

"I'm not planning to."

"I think you should."

Providencia   *Deborah A. Hodge*

"Why?"

"I would like to be sure that you are over him and that you could open all of your heart to me."

"I can do that without seeing him."

"I'm not so sure."

"What if I don't want to see him?"

"That concerns me greatly."

"Why?"

"Because you wouldn't go out with me for three years and it was because of him, right?"

"Yes," Sarah answered reluctantly.

"So you were hoping to get back with him," Christian said.

"I didn't know. We put it in God's hands. I didn't know what God had in mind."

"So I was a fall back," Christian added.

"You weren't a fall back. I hadn't heard from him and nothing had changed as far as God's leading. Therefore, I thought maybe you might be God's choice for me."

Christian made her look him straight in the eyes. "Am I?"

Sarah's eyes narrowed and her face betrayed her uncertainty. "I think so."

Christian clenched his teeth. "But, you don't know for sure. Do you?"

With an unchanged face, Sarah echoed her previous answer. "I think so."

"I want you to be certain. I want you to see Jason while he's here."

"I don't know about that. I'll have to think about it."

The talk with Christian had unnerved her. She had tried to be certain

Chapter 8

that he was the one. She had prayed about it repeatedly. God hadn't said no, but she wasn't sure He had said yes. She had grown tired of waiting on Jason and she knew that Christian was a good and godly man. Surely God approved of him, but she wasn't sure that He approved of her agreeing to marry him.

When she returned home from her talk with Christian, her parents could tell that she was upset. She walked to the living room and collapsed in a chair. They decided to venture a conversation.

"How'd it go?" her dad asked.

"I don't know."

"If you don't mind me asking, what happened?" her mother inquired.

"Christian wants me to see Jason while he's here."

"He does," her mother responded.

"What do you want to do?" her dad asked.

Sarah stared into space. "I don't know."

"Why did Christian want you to see Jason?" her mother asked.

"I think he's afraid I'm still in love with Jason."

"Are you?" her mom asked.

"I don't know. I haven't seen him in four years. As far as I know, nothing's changed concerning God's will for him and me."

"How do you know? He is in Ecuador after all," her mom pointed out.

"He's on a mission trip. He didn't come for me."

"How do you know?" her mom asked.

Sarah stared at her. "Why would you ask that?"

Her dad moved to the edge of his chair. "She's asking because she loves you."

"Dad, I don't think his being here has anything to do with me."

Her mother mused aloud. "God sometimes surprises us. Maybe that's what He's doing."

Providencia   *Deborah A. Hodge*

Her dad shifted in his chair. "What if Jason is here for you?"

Sarah sighed, shook her head and answered, "I don't think he is."

"But what if he is?"

"I don't know."

"Do you still love him?"

Sarah agonized, "I don't know. I've tried not to think about it. I never expected to see him again."

"Christian is wise to want you to see Jason."

"I don't want to hurt Christian. I promised to marry him."

"That wouldn't be fair to him if you love another man."

"I'm not sure I do."

"But you'll never know unless you see Jason."

Sarah closed her eyes and sighed deeply. "What about Christian?"

"Put it all in God hands like you've done before."

"Dad, I don't understand this. Why is God doing this to me?"

"What do you think He's doing to you?"

"Just when I think I've figured things out, He keeps pulling the rug out from under me."

"That's when we have to trust him the most."

"Sarah, God has always taken care of us. He has always been faithful. He's always kept His promises. You know that," her mother reminded.

"I trusted Him, let Jason go, and came to Ecuador. I hoped that things would change, but Jason never called, wrote, emailed or came for four years. I trusted Him when I accepted Christian's proposal and now, Jason is coming to Ecuador. I don't understand."

"That's why you pray, trust Him and see Jason. God will make things clear as you trust Him," her dad said.

Chapter 8

Sarah reluctantly agreed, prayed with her parents, and put it all in God's hands. She talked to Christian again, trying to convince him that she shouldn't see Jason, but he continued to believe as her parents did that she should see him. She and Christian prayed and committed the whole thing to the Lord. She continued to pray, hoping the Lord would say no to her going to Quito, but He didn't. She didn't get it. Everyone seemed to be pushing her toward Jason. She seemingly had no real choice in the matter so she reluctantly made plans to go to Quito to see Jason when he arrived.

In the midst of making plans, Rodrigo, a friend she had grown up with, called her to see whether she could serve as a translator for the very mission team Jason was bringing to Ecuador. She saw this as the providence of God and began to believe that maybe God was surprising her. Maybe God had brought Jason to Ecuador for her.

The first night at the airport, as Jason walked toward her, recognized her and froze as if he had seen a ghost, she was surprised all right. It was apparent that he was not expecting to see her. He had not come to Ecuador for her.

Christian's unexpected appearance at the airport that night served to confuse her even more. She thought that maybe he had come to get a glimpse of the competition, and maybe he had. However, he told her that he was there to reinforce his willingness to leave their future in God's hands. As she hugged him goodbye, she felt torn between the present and the past, and anxious about the future.

Even though she gave Christian a smile as he walked away, she wasn't smiling inside. It was all she could do to keep it together. "God, what are you doing to me? It is evident that this man loves me, and the man standing over there doesn't even want me to be here."

Providencia   *Deborah A. Hodge*

This particular day had been an enigma also. The cordial words between them as he searched for her lunch had caused her to hope, and then two minutes later Jason shot all that down with his stiff reply. Sarah decided to give it time. She prayed. "Please God help me understand what's going on. I want to be in the center of Your will."

Roy's call for everyone to gather around interrupted her prayer. She was not at all prepared for what he was about to say.

"We are going back out to witness some more, but we need to tweak the teams a little."

He called the new teams out, and Sarah's heart skipped a beat as she heard her name paired with Jason's team. Sarah realized that there must have been an outward reaction when Katty asked, "Is everything okay?"

Embarrassed, Sarah struggled for a quick response. "Everything is fine."

"Are you sure? Is there a problem with your assignment?"

Sarah shook her head. "No, the assignment is fine."

"Good, I suggested that Roy pair you with Jason's team because we have a new translator, Luz Gutierrez. She has never translated. She had some difficulty this morning. I wanted her to listen and learn from you. If that's not okay, I can go with Jason and let you go with Roy again."

Sarah knew this was a moment of decision when she had to trust God and His providence. "It's fine. I'll be glad to go with Jason's group and help Luz."

She shot a glance in Jason's direction and saw that he was talking to Roy. She saw him glance in her direction a couple of times. It appeared

Chapter 9

that she wasn't the only one who had misgivings about the team assignments, but even if that was so, nothing changed.

Jason motioned for his team. "Let's be going."

Sarah and the others quickly gathered their things and followed.

Sarah introduced herself to Luz as they began. "Hola, I am Sarah Barnes. You must be Luz."

"I am. It is nice to meet you Sarah. I learn from you, sí?"

"Sí."

She noticed Jason glance over his shoulder and she knew he was listening to the conversation. She wondered if she should avoid conversation in his presence. That became impossible because of Luz's curiosity.

"How long have you been translator?" she asked.

"I'm not a translator. I'm a nurse."

"Then why are you here?"

She saw Jason glance over his shoulder again as she answered. "I'm here because Katty needed another translator and a mutual friend of ours asked me to."

"Oh, I see. I am here to improve English."

Sarah smiled. "You already speak reasonably good English."

"Thank you, but I want to learn to hear it well as well as speak. Translating should help to do that."

"You're right. You are Colombian, yes?" Sarah inquired.

"Sí, I am; my family came to Ecuador several years ago to escape drug violence."

"I see."

"You are Ecuadorian," Luz observed.

"No, I am American, but I have lived most of my life in Ecuador. My parents are missionaries."

"I see. My parents are shopkeepers here in Quito."

"Do you have brothers and sisters?"

"I have one brother, but my brother has returned to Colombia. He was older when we came to Ecuador, and he missed friends so when he became old enough he returned. My parents are very sad because of this. They worry for Eduardo."

"I am sorry for your parent's sadness."

"They have great faith in God. They committed my brother into His hands."

"They are very wise."

In listening to the conversation Jason hadn't uncovered anything different from what the old Sarah would have said. That boggled his mind. She must have changed. She couldn't be the same Sarah and be marrying someone else. That couldn't happen. He took a good look at her as he walked by her side. Her long brown hair, big brown eyes, brilliant smile, tan skin, all accenting her slim, well-portioned frame made her more beautiful than he remembered. She seemed to be as personable and outgoing as ever. He knew he was in danger of loving her more than he ever had, but the diamond ring on her left hand told him that he couldn't allow himself to. *God help me. You know what I'm feeling. I give the situation to You.* His thoughts were interrupted as he spied a man and woman sitting outside their house.

"Let's stop here."

Jason led the team toward the couple. "Hola," he greeted.

"Hola," they greeted.

Jason glanced toward Sarah. "Please tell them that we are missionaries from the United States sent by God to share the gospel with the people of Ecuador."

Sarah complied with flawless Spanish and a beautiful smile. The couple smiled and nodded their understanding.

"Please tell them our names."

Sarah introduced everyone to the couple and the couple responded with their names, Orlando and Enez. Jason smiled and repeated the couple's names.

Chapter 9

"Please ask them if they know they will go to heaven when they die."

Sarah did as he asked, and both responded that they did not know for sure that they would go to heaven, but they hoped so. They said they were trying to be good enough that God would let them in.

"Ask them if they would like to know for sure that they will go to heaven when they die."

Sarah asked, and the couple nodded. Jason shared the gospel of how God sent His Son Jesus to die on the cross in mankind's place to pay for all sins, so that anyone who accepts Jesus as their personal Savior and Lord can be forgiven. He explained that salvation through Jesus' atoning work on the cross makes it possible for a person to know for sure that he or she will go to Heaven to be with Him for eternity. Sarah translated with precision and tenderness.

As Jason came to the point of invitation, he asked, "God offers each of you a personal invitation to accept Jesus as your personal Savior. Would either of you like to ask Jesus to forgive you of your sins and become your personal Savior and Lord?"

Sarah translated and Orlando and Enez nodded. Jason looked at Sarah. "Why don't you lead them in a sinner's prayer? You know exactly what to say," he smiled as he continued, "and you can say it better than I."

Sarah smiled, nodded and led Orlando and Enez in the sinner's prayer. They joyfully repeated every word. As they finished the prayer, the expressions of joy on their faces gave proof to the validity of their salvation. They smiled broadly and began shaking hands and hugging team members.

"Sarah, please invite them to the services at the mission church at 7 p.m. tonight."

Sarah complied and the couple nodded and promised to be there.

Jason thrust forth his hand. "Dios te bendiga."

"You speak Spanish," Luz said.

Jason cut his eyes toward Sarah, who had been his teacher all those years ago. She looked down. Jason smiled at Luz. "I know a little."

The team said goodbye and continued in search of others with whom they could share the gospel. They continued to stop and share for the

---

Providencia　　　　　　　　　　　　　　　　　*Deborah A. Hodge*

next two hours. Their efforts resulted in sixteen professions of faith.

As they walked back toward the buses, Luz voiced her amazement. "I cannot believe how simple it is to share the gospel. I have always thought that it was hard. I thought that I did not know enough of the Bible to do it."

Jason smiled. "The only thing you have to know is Jesus. If you have a personal relationship with Him, you just tell others how He saved you and that they can have what you have."

"I see," Luz smiled and contemplated. "Why did you ask them about heaven?"

"Because many people count on good works to get them into heaven, but that will never do it. God sent Jesus to make a way for people to go to heaven. Belief in Him and His atoning death is the only way to be right with God."

"I think I see," Luz said. "Sarah you did so well translating. I am not sure I can do that."

"Sure you can," Sarah encouraged.

"I don't know. I don't think I can hear English and translate it into Spanish that quickly."

Sarah smiled. "You might have to practice a little, but I'm sure that you can."

"She's right. Sarah, you did a fantastic job," said Cannon, whose group had teamed up with Jason's for the day.

Without looking directly at her, Jason agreed. "They're right; you did."

Sarah blushed. "Thanks, but I just said, what you said."

Jason's face took on an expression of concern as he joked. "I hope so."

Sarah looked worried until everyone laughed.

Chapter 9

Providencia *Deborah A. Hodge*

Things were different after that day. Jason began to act more like the old Jason and Sarah knew she was in danger of loving him more than ever. It also became apparent over the next few days that Luz was enamored with Jason too. Sarah had watched as Luz gazed adoringly at Jason and drank in every word, every smile, and every laugh. She knew the signs of infatuation, and Luz had it bad.

Luz followed Jason around like a lovesick teenager. Actually, that's exactly what she was, a lovesick girl of eighteen. Everyone recognized her infatuation with Jason, except Jason. Sarah could see that it particularly perturbed Rachael.

Sarah watched the unfolding drama day after day and its exacerbation of Rachael's jealousy. Meals were especially onerous as Sarah sat with Rachael. Sarah was witness to all of Rachael's moods, triggered by what was happening two tables over. Though she could not voice it, Sarah identified with Rachael's jealousy as she steamed over Luz's flirting with Jason as they ate breakfast.

Sarah knew Jason well enough to know that even though he laughed at her antics he was unaware that Luz was flirting. Sarah was amazed at how naïve he seemed to be and was unaware that she was shaking her head until she heard Rachael say, "I agree."

"What?"

"You were shaking your head at the little scene. Weren't you?"

Embarrassed, Sarah answered sheepishly. "I guess I was."

Rachael let out a huff. "It amazes me how a level-headed guy like Jay can act so childish."

Rachael dropped her fork and shook her head. "Look at him. Someone

Chapter 10

needs to explain to him that he doesn't need to encourage Luz."

Sarah paused from eating her pancakes, as she watched the activities two tables over. "I don't think he even knows what's going on."

"I tried to point it out to him last night, but he just laughed," Rachael said.

"Why did he laugh?" Sarah asked.

"Because you're right, he doesn't have a clue."

"What did he say when you told him?"

"He said she's a baby. I told him that he'd better take another look. She's a Latin beauty with long brown hair, big brown eyes and a crush on you."

Sarah agreed completely, but she wouldn't admit it aloud. She worked hard to hide any hint of her own jealousy. She played with her breakfast and asked, "What did he say?"

"He laughed and played it off."

Sarah jumped as Rachael placed her coffee cup loudly on the table and propped her hands on her hips. "What's wrong with him? How could he be so blind?"

A stranger diverted Sarah's attention from the conversation. "Who's that with Luz and Jason?"

"I don't know."

Roy walked up as they watched Luz hugging the tall stranger tightly. He had joined them in their observation.

"Sure looks like Luz knows him," Rachael observed.

"Maybe he's Luz's boyfriend, and we've been wrong about her crush on Jason."

Rachael and Sarah looked at each other. "I don't think so," Rachael said.

They continued to watch as Luz took Jason's hand and arm as she introduced the young man to him.

Providencia   *Deborah A. Hodge*

"Maybe she likes both of them," Roy chimed in, taking a seat.

"Maybe, but someone should set Jason straight."

"He won't listen to me. Maybe he'll listen to one of you girls."

Rachael leaned back, folded her arms and said, "Not me. He'll just think I'm being jealous. It'll have to be Sarah." Twinges of jealousy shot through Sarah as she heard Rachael's remark about being jealous.

"And he'd be right, wouldn't he?" Roy observed.

"Me jealous ... of Luz?" Rachael barked as she slid to the front of her seat, clenched her jaw, gritted her teeth, and shook her head.

Roy spoke bluntly. "Forgive me, Rachael, but you get green-eyed every time a good looking girl talks to Jason. I'm surprised you're so friendly with Sarah."

Sarah's head spun around at that comment. She was stunned.

Rachael sought a quick remedy for her embarrassment. "Don't pay any attention to Roy. He doesn't know what he's talking about."

Sarah knew better. She knew Rachael had a thing for Jason. She also knew by the interrogations she had received from Rachael that she had been jealous of her until Luz came along and changed her focus.

Roy clucked with amazement. "How long have you worked for Jason and me?"

"A little over a year."

Roy looked Rachael straight in the eyes. "And, how long have you been in love with Jason?"

Sarah swallowed hard as she waited for Rachael's answer. Rachael glared at Roy but didn't answer.

Amused by Rachael's response, Roy answered his own question. "About a year."

Rachael folded her arms and huffed, "Surely I can't be that obvious."

Roy laughed. "Only to those of us who know you've been chasing him for the past year."

Rachael was not amused. "I can't believe you said that. I haven't been

Chapter 10

chasing him."

Roy grinned. "Yeah right."

Sarah shifted in her chair. *There is definitely something going on. I knew it.*

Rachael bristled with anger.

Roy backed off. "Calm down. Can't you take a little kidding?"

Rachael shot back, "Not about that. I don't think it's very funny."

"I'm sorry. I didn't mean to hurt your feelings."

Luz interrupted Roy's apology as she, the tall stranger and Jason came over.

Luz smiled. "I would like to introduce to you my brother, Eduardo."

Everyone smiled and said hello.

Luz motioned toward each one as she continued, "Eduardo, this is Sarah, Rachael and Roy. They are also missionaries from the U.S. States."

"It is nice to meet you. Thank you for being so kind to my sister."

Roy smiled. "You are most welcome. Your sister has been a Godsend."

"He's right," Jason agreed as he put his arm around Luz's shoulder. "She's become a wonderful translator. We are lucky to have her."

Eduardo cocked his head. "She speaks well of you, also. She tells me that you are a professor at a prestigious seminary in Kansas."

Jason pointed to Roy. "Roy is also a professor there."

"Two professors," Eduardo said.

"They are leaders of the group," Luz proudly pointed out. She motioned toward Sarah. "Sarah is the one who taught me to be translator."

"You are Ecuadorian?" Eduardo inquired.

"I am American, but I have lived here most of my life. My parents are missionaries in Peguche."

"I see. You are very lovely and could be mistaken for Ecuadorian."

Providencia   *Deborah A. Hodge*

Sarah blushed. "Thank you."

Luz smiled. "He is only saying truth, and I think you are Ecuadorian at heart."

"She certainly has Ecuador in her heart," Jason said.

Sarah glanced to see whether the comment was sarcasm or an honest observation. Her glance did not help her discern the meaning of the comment. She decided to let it go.

Luz turned her attention to Rachael. "Rachael is Roy and Jason's secretary."

Rachael smiled an unenthusiastic smile.

"Another lovely lady," Eduardo quipped.

"Wow, I like your brother, Luz."

"He does have a good tongue." Everyone laughed. "Did I not say correctly?"

"What were you trying to say?" Sarah asked.

Luz answered her in Spanish. Sarah smiled. "I think you mean he has a silver tongue. He knows how to speak well, how to interact with people well."

"Yes, that is what I mean. Thank you."

Eduardo smiled. "My sister speaks too well of me."

"She is proud of you. Sisters are like that," Roy said.

"You have a sister?" Eduardo inquired.

"I have two."

"And you Jason, do you have sisters?"

"No it's just me. I'm an only child and my parents died when I was a boy."

"I did not know that about you," Luz said, as she put her arm around Jason.

Sarah glanced at Rachael. The green-eyed monster had taken up

Chapter 10

residence in her blue eyes. Sarah didn't know which should concern her most, Luz's infatuation or Rachael's obvious feelings for Jason.

Eduardo was not pleased with his sister's obvious familiarity with Jason. He spoke plainly, "Señor Jason, I think that you are the one with the silver tongue. My sister hangs on your every word."

This time Jason blushed.

Eduardo continued, "She has never been happier. Her face lights up every time she speaks of you and the possibility of going to school in North America."

Roy rubbed his chin, as he trolled for more information. "So you might be coming to America, Luz?"

Luz enthusiastically answered, "Maybe. Jason says he might know someone who will sponsor me and help me go to university in Kansas."

With a clenched jaw and green eyes, Rachael added, "How nice."

"It is very nice. It will change my life if it is so," Luz said.

She gripped Jason's arm tighter as she looked up at him. Her admiration and infatuation were unmistakable to everyone except Jason. The green-eyed monster in Rachael's eyes had hit overdrive. With arms folded, jaw tight and teeth clenched, Rachael crossed her legs, swinging them nervously.

Eduardo was very displeased at his little sister's statement. "Yes, it will change her life and my parents' also; you are their only daughter."

Jason heard his concern and tried to reassure him. "If things work out for Luz to come to the U.S., she will only be gone long enough to go to college. They will see her again."

"That may be true, but they will be sad at her leaving."

Luz protested, "You left, Eduardo, and you are their only son."

"You are right, but I am in Colombia and it is a short journey away."

Luz upbraided him. "If it is such a short journey why has it taken you two years to return?"

"I am a grown man and I have business to take care of."

Luz stomped her foot. "Am I not a grown woman?"

Providencia   Deborah A. Hodge

Eduardo's anger flared. He pointed at Luz as he spoke and then to Jason. "You think you are grown. I am not so sure. Your head can be turned by promises made by a man that you have known but a week."

Anger flooded Luz's face. "Eduardo, you are very rude."

Eduardo's comment flustered Jason into defending his integrity. "Eduardo, I can assure you that I do not make promises lightly. I promised your sister that I would try to help her and I will."

Eduardo brushed his hair from his eyes, stood erect and spoke with great conviction. "Maybe that is so, but I cannot support my sister going to America. I do not like your country."

That statement brought an immediate rise out of Rachael. "And just what is wrong with our country?"

Eduardo answered forcefully. "Your country tries to force others to do as it says. It is very imperialistic."

"Eduardo! Do not speak to my friends this way. They did not come here for politics, but for God."

"Sí, yes, they came to share American Christianity and to deceive our people."

Roy, Rachael and Sarah held their breath. They wondered what Jason would say. They had watched Jason's face reveal distinct irritation as Eduardo had begun his tirade. Upon hearing Eduardo's last comment, he briefly closed his eyes before he responded.

"Eduardo, we did not come here to spread American Christianity, and certainly not to deceive anyone. We came here to spread God's good news of God's love to all people. We came to tell the people of Ecuador that because God loves them He sent His son to die for their sins that they might have a right relationship with Him through Jesus."

Eduardo shot back, "Colombian Christianity teaches that Jesus died to make men free and that God wants all men to be treated equal and not live under oppression."

Roy observed, "I think you are expressing a belief in a type of liberation theology."

Very defensively, Eduardo blurted, "I am speaking of true Christianity, Colombian Christianity."

Jason had closed his eyes briefly again. Sarah was sure he was praying. Finally, he spoke: "Jesus did die to make men free, free from sin, and fit for a relationship with him. God loves us, but He does not promise us heaven on earth. He does not promise justice in this life, but He does promise us justice. The Bible says that one day all people will stand before Him and give an account for the deeds done during their lives."

Eduardo's eyes flashed as he shifted his feet and moved toward Jason. "I have been taught that God does not want us to wait. He expects us to help achieve His justice by fighting oppression now."

Luz bolted toward Eduardo. "Eduardo, go now! It is obvious that you want to argue, not talk."

Jason intervened. "It's okay, Luz."

Luz shook her head. "It is not okay. He has been this way all of life. He listens to no one. He knows everything."

With a rigid stance and anger in his eyes, Eduardo replied, "I know you are being brainwashed by these Americans."

"That is not true!" Luz shouted so loudly that everyone in the cafeteria stared. Eduardo seemed to enjoy being the center of attention. He shouted back. "It is true."

Roy stood up and Katty walked over as Jason interjected, "Let's all calm down. We can talk it out."

Eduardo shifted his feet again and spoke with great force, "I do not wish to talk it out. I wish to take my sister home."

Luz backed away. "But, I do not wish to go."

Eduardo grabbed her arm. "You are coming with me."

Luz jerked her arm away. "I am not." Eduardo lunged toward her. Roy and Jason stopped him.

"Look man, I don't want to interfere in family business, but it's obvious that she doesn't want to go with you," Jason said.

Katty came to Luz's rescue by speaking in Spanish to Eduardo. Eduardo backed up and walked away. Tears flowed from Luz's eyes as she watched him leave. Jason gently wrapped his arm around her and tried to console her. Luz buried her face in his shoulder.

Providencia   *Deborah A. Hodge*

"What did you say to him?" Roy asked.

Sarah answered, "She said that she believed him to be a member of FARC and that she would report him if he continued to create a disturbance."

"What is FARC?" Rachael asked.

"It is the Revolutionary Armed Forces of Colombia, a rebel group that claims to fight for the poor against the rich and powerful," Katty explained. "They are how you say, Marxista."

Sarah translated. "They are Marxists."

Katty nodded. "Sí, they are Marxists and are trying to overthrow Colombia's government."

Luz raised her head from Jason's shoulder and protested, "My brother is not a member of FARC."

"Maybe not, but he sure acted like it," Katty said.

Tears streaming again, Luz repeated, "He is not a member of FARC. He is not."

Jason patted her back. "It's all right."

Luz wiped tears, and repeated, "He is not."

Katty put her hand on Luz's arm to comfort her. "I'm sorry. I did not mean to upset you. I only meant to calm the situation."

Luz nodded, wiped more tears and forced a smiled. "Okay."

"Well, we need to round everyone up, make assignments and get on the bus," Roy suggested.

That statement ended the scene and everyone gathered, received their assignments, walked to the buses and traveled to a new area. The day ended on a better note as they experienced another wonderful day of seeing God work in people's hearts and lives.

Providencia   *Deborah A. Hodge*

Throughout the next week, Luz served as the translator for Jason's group. Sarah realized that Luz's crush on Jason seemed to deepen. She stayed close to him, hung on his every word and often walked beside him while grasping his arm.

Sarah stayed back, prayed, checked on Luz's translation skills, and observed the interaction between Jason and Luz. She was amazed at how truly oblivious Jason was to what was happening. Sarah knew that he would never intentionally lead Luz on, but Luz was truly head over heels with infatuation for him.

The other team members had begun to notice and whisper about some kind of relationship between Jason and Luz.

Rachael voiced her fury. "Sarah, someone has to do something."

"What do you mean?"

"I've overheard the seminary students talking and laughing about Jason and Luz."

"Really."

"I'm afraid so."

Sarah shook her head. "What are they saying?"

"They're talking about how Professor Jay has found himself a beautiful young Ecuadorian girlfriend who has the hots for him, and wondering why they hadn't realized that he was such a player."

Sarah frowned. "Jason's not a player."

Rachael let out a huff. "Don't I know it, but he sure looks like one with

Chapter 11

Luz."

"I'm sorry. I know this must be hard for you."

"Yeah, Roy kind of let the cat out of the bag, didn't he?"

Working hard to hide her own jealousy, Sarah forced a grin. "Yeah. Anyway it's very evident that you have feelings for Jason."

"Good, then I can be overt. He makes me so mad. I am livid."

Sarah wrinkled her brow. "Livid?"

Rachael gritted her teeth. "Livid! I am furious with Jason!"

"Jason?"

Rachael stomped her foot. "Yes Jason. I can understand what Luz sees in him, He's kind, thoughtful, has those amazing deep blue eyes, but I can't understand how he can be so blind to her infatuation with him."

Sarah nodded in agreement. "From my past experience with Jason, he has a one-track mind. He's thinking about the objectives of this trip, not about romance."

With arms folded and jaw clenched, Rachael spewed out her opinion. "Well, he needs to stop encouraging her. He makes me so mad holding her hand and constantly hugging her."

Sarah felt the same way but couldn't voice it. "Yeah, well someone needs to talk to him."

"I've tried to, and Roy's tried to. I think you should try."

Sarah could feel her heart quicken at that statement. She swallowed hard and said, "I'm not sure I should do that."

"Why not? I think he'd listen to you."

Sarah's eyes widened. "Why would he listen to me if he hasn't listened to you or Roy?"

Rachael cocked her head. "Because you are friends with Luz … and him."

Sarah's eyes widened again. "I just met Luz, and Jason and I used to be friends."

Providencia　　　　　　　　　　　　　　　　*Deborah A. Hodge*

"That may be true, but I have seen how they both respect you and your opinion."

"I don't think I ought to be the one."

Rachael folded her arms, stood erect, and stared for a moment. "Look Sarah, he won't listen to Roy. He won't listen to me. He thinks I'm being jealous. He knows you're not jealous. You're engaged to Christian."

Sarah was silent for a moment. How wrong Rachael was, but Sarah couldn't admit it.

Rachael peppered her again. "Please Sarah. He's making a fool of himself and he needs to know it."

Sarah reluctantly agreed. "Okay, I'll do it, but I'm not sure I'll do any good."

At the end of each day the teams had services at the cooperating churches. Some members preached, some sang. The services helped to re-energize both the church members and the team members. After the services, the teams gathered back to the seminary cafeteria to share the day's experiences and thank God for His presence.

That night after the team gathering concluded, Sarah decided to speak to Jason about Luz.

Haltingly and with wringing hands behind her back, Sarah walked up to Jason and uttered her request, "Jason, may I talk to you about something?"

She sensed that he seemed a little uncomfortable at the prospect. She heard a slight stutter as he answered, "Yeah, sure."

Sarah pointed to one of the tables in the dimly lit area of the cafeteria. "Could we sit over there?"

Jason frowned, chewed his lip, and followed her slowly.

As they sat down, he jumped in with authority, "What's up?"

Sarah began without looking directly at him. "I don't know how to say this, but to simply speak plainly."

"Okay, let's hear it."

Chapter 11

Sarah fidgeted in her chair. "I need to talk to you about Luz."

As she looked up to see his reaction, he let out his breath and sounded slightly irritated as he asked. "What about Luz?"

"Jason, she's head over heels in love with you."

Jason laughed. "Not you, too."

"Yes, me too, since you haven't listened to anyone else, I thought I'd give it a try."

"Luz is a sweet kid, and I'm simply being nice to her."

"Luz is a young woman who is in love with her "knight in shining armor."

His mouth flew open, and he laughed. "You have to be kidding."

"I'm not. Everyone sees it but you."

Jason smirked and shook his head. "Rachael put you up to this, didn't she?"

"Not exactly."

Jason sat up in his chair. "Look, I've already had a lecture from Roy and Rachael. I don't need one from you. Luz is just a nice, friendly young girl. You're all wrong."

"We're not wrong. She is nice, but she's not that young. And, she certainly is way too friendly. That was the main reason her brother was so upset."

Jason's eyes widened. "That's absurd."

"I'm afraid it's not, and you also need to know that your relationship with Luz has become a topic of gossip."

Jason's eyes popped and his mouth flew open. This time he didn't laugh. "What!"

Sarah nodded. "I'm sorry, but it's true. I thought you should know."

Jason closed his eyes and shook his head. "I'm still not convinced about Luz, but I don't like being gossiped about, especially since I haven't done anything wrong. Nevertheless, you're right; I do need to do something about the situation. What do you suggest that I do?"

Providencia   *Deborah A. Hodge*

"Back off a little, don't let her hug you so much or hold your hand so much. Pay attention to someone else. She'll get the message."

She watched as a sudden look of realization swept over his face. "Wow, I *have* been doing that, haven't I?"

Compassion shone through her eyes as Sarah nodded. "Uh–huh."

Jason dropped his head and distress dripped from his voice. "I really have been sending her the wrong signal, haven't I?"

"I'm afraid so."

"I swear I didn't mean to; I didn't realize I was doing it. I wasn't thinking about her that way."

Without consciously realizing it, Sarah touched his arm. "I know."

Jason lifted his head slightly and voiced his concern. "How do I back off without hurting her?" He sighed. "I don't want to hurt her."

Sarah placed her hand on his arm. "Put some space between you and her; assign her to another group."

Jason put his hand over hers. "I'm not sure she'll understand and I don't want to hurt her."

Sarah looked into his eyes. "I'm not sure that can be helped."

As their eyes met momentarily, feelings from the past took over. Each quickly looked away and withdrew the offending hands.

Sarah tried not to make eye contact as she cleared her throat. "Yeah, well I know you'll do the right thing now that you know the truth."

"Yeah, I will. Thanks for telling me."

"You're welcome," Sarah said.

From his vantage point, Jason could see someone enter the door of the cafeteria. "Isn't that your fiancé?"

Sarah leaned over to see. "Yes, it is." She motioned for Christian to come over.

Christian swiftly obliged. Sarah rose to greet him with a hug. Jason

Chapter 11

watched.

"Christian, this is Jason Parks, an old friend from Kansas. Jason this is Christian Romero, my fiancé."

Jason had stood as the introduction began and both men thrust their hands forward. They shook hands without trying to measure which one had a firmer grasp.

"Nice to meet you, Christian."

"And you, Jason," Christian said as he turned his attention to Sarah. "Sarah I came to tell you about Rio."

Sarah's eyes flashed with great concern. "Rio, what's wrong?"

"He is not responding to the medicine as he was. I knew that you would want to know."

"What are you going to do?"

"I am trying a different medicine and asking Dr. Munoz to consult."

"Do you think he will?"

"He has promised to drive back with me tonight."

"Who's with Rio now?"

"Majo."

Sarah breathed a sigh of relief. "He is in good hands."

"Yes, he is," Christian agreed, "but he asked to see you."

Sarah bit her lip and touched her mouth with the back of her hand. "He did?"

Christian smiled. "He did. Would you like to go tonight? I will bring you back tomorrow."

Sarah looked at Jason. "Rio is a five-year-old boy in our mission hospital. He has a rare lung disease. His parents are dead and he lives with his grandmother. Since he's been in the hospital, we've bonded."

Jason smiled as she explained. "So go see Rio."

"I know that will leave you short-handed."

Providencia   *Deborah A. Hodge*

"We'll cope. Go see Rio."

Sarah's face flashed a bright smile. "Thanks, Jason."

Christian echoed, "Thanks, Jason."

"No problem."

"I promise I'll have her back tomorrow afternoon."

Sarah smiled again and took Christian's arm. "See you tomorrow."

Jason nodded. "Yeah, see you."

As Jason watched her turn and walk away, he sighed and with his elbows on the table rubbed his face with his hands. *Help me Father. It's killing me to see her with someone else.*

Providencia   *Deborah A. Hodge*

Rachael had been in the shadows watching and listening to the whole thing from a corner nearby. She had wanted to see how Jason would react when Sarah opened his eyes about Luz. However, Rachael's eyes were the ones opened as she watched Jason and Sarah interact. Christian's entrance only tantalized her suspicions more. With Christian and Sarah's exit, she decided to talk to Jason.

"How you doing?" she asked, as she sat down.

Jason dropped his hands and blew out a deep breath. "Great, I'm doing great. It's been quite a day."

"And quite a night."

"What does that mean?"

Rachael folded her arms. "I saw you with Sarah."

"She was explaining to me about Luz."

"Yeah, I know, but I also know what I saw."

Jason cocked his head. "And what did you see?"

"I saw enough to know that I should be more jealous of Sarah than Luz."

Jason stared at her without saying a word.

Rachael wouldn't let it go. "She *is* your ghost, isn't she? She's the girl you were talking about on the plane."

Jason clenched his jaw but didn't answer.

"You might as well admit it. I know it's true. She went to school in

Chapter 12

Kansas. She's granddaughter of John Jones. It all fits."

Jason sighed and dropped his head in frustration. "Okay, I'll admit it. She's the one."

"So what happened?"

"You saw what happened. She left with Christian."

"I'm not talking about that and you know it."

Jason shook his head in frustration. "Yeah, I know."

"So what happened with Sarah and you?"

Jason let out a deep sigh but remained silent.

"If you don't tell me, I'll worm it out of her."

Jason's head shot up. "No, don't do that. I'll tell you." He took a deep breath and plunged in.

"Sarah and I were engaged."

Rachael's mouth flew open, "Engaged!"

Jason nodded.

"What happened? How come she's here and you're in Kansas?"

"God led me in one direction and her in another and so we called the whole thing off."

Rachael sighed as she made an inquiry that she really didn't want to make. "But you still love her, don't you?"

Jason looked away. Rachael had her answer, but she asked again. "You do, don't you?"

This time Jason nodded. "I do. I've tried not to, but I do."

Rachael looked away. She couldn't help the jealousy that surfaced. She tried hard not to allow it to control her response. She prayed as she searched for the right thing to say. *God help me do and say the right thing.* She glanced at Jason; she could see the pain on his face. Finally, the words came. "She's a great girl. Why shouldn't you love her?"

Jason stared at Rachael. "I don't get you. A while ago, you talked about being jealous; I don't understand where you are coming from."

"I was jealous; I am jealous, but it's one thing to be jealous of an eighteen-year-old who has a crush on you. It's quite another to be jealous of someone whom you obviously love and who loves you, especially if she is as fantastic a person as Sarah is. I can't compete with that. I accept defeat. Therefore, I repeat, why shouldn't you love her?"

He sighed deeply. "I can't love her. She's engaged to another man, and my ministry is in Kansas and hers is in Ecuador. I can't love her."

Rachael touched his hand. He turned his head and looked at her. "But you do, and you should tell her how you feel."

"I can't. We broke up because God had called us to two different places and that hasn't changed."

Rachael jiggled his hand. "One thing has changed. You are both in the same place now, and I think she still loves you too."

Jason shook his head. "Yeah right, that's why she's wearing Christian's ring and why she left with him tonight."

"If I overheard correctly, she left to see a five-year-old boy named Rio, and I'll bet if you'd tell her how you feel, she'd give the ring back."

Jason's face and body language revealed his irritation. "You don't know what you're talking about. She doesn't love me anymore."

Rachael's eyes narrowed as she admonished Jason. "I was eavesdropping, remember? And I heard and saw what went on between you and Sarah before Christian arrived. I'm not wrong about how Sarah feels about you." She looked him squarely in the eyes. "Jason, you need to tell her how you feel."

"That's not fair to her or Christian."

"At least think about it and pray about it."

"I've prayed about it and thought about it for four years. Nothing has changed."

Rachael shook her head at Jason's pain. She took his hands in hers and smiled. "At least now I understand why I never stood a chance with you." She forced Jason to smile back. It was a half-hearted smile, but it was a smile.

Jason looked at his watch. "We'd better turn in. Six o'clock will come early."

After he left the cafeteria the night before, Jason found a spot on the seminary grounds where he could be alone with God, and he poured his heart out in prayer. On his knees, heart breaking and tears flowing, he held nothing back. "Father, You know that I want nothing more than to do Your will. I don't know what to do here. I don't know how to handle this. Evidently, I'm letting my feelings show. Rachael sees it; maybe Sarah does too. Please help me know what to do. For four years, I have trusted you concerning Sarah and the future. Even though I have given her to you repeatedly, she has never left my heart. I love her as much as I always have, maybe more. She's lovelier than I remembered, and she radiates Your love even more than she did. I see that you have continued to do a deep work in her life. Father, all of this makes her even more attractive to me, but I know she's still unattainable. She's forgotten the past; she's marrying another man. God please help me to move on, too. Please, please help me." After more tears from the very depth of his soul, he concluded, "Father I want to be your man, your minister, your preacher, and I want to leave every aspect of my life in Your hands. I do that now." Before he rose from his knees, he remembered, "Father please help me with Luz too. Give me the wisdom to know how to handle the situation with her. In Jesus' name, I pray. Amen."

Rising, he looked up and marveled at the night sky adorned with hundreds of brilliant diamonds. The magnificent starlit heavens gave him comfort. The God who created such grandeur could handle any problems he had. He stood silently praising God for Who He was and for having heard Him as he had poured out his heart.

He peeked at his watch as he entered his quarters. He couldn't believe that he only had four hours until he had to get up. He fell into bed and slept soundly until his alarm awakened him.

When he reached the cafeteria, Rachael waved for him to sit beside

Chapter 13

her. With no way out, he picked up his breakfast tray and joined her. Immediately, she began, "How are you?"

Even though he knew she meant well, Rachael's question did not sit well. He was not very open to her concern.

"I'm fine," Jason answered as he took a bite of his banana.

Holding her coffee cup in her hands, she paused before she took a sip. "Did you sleep well?"

Swallowing a spoon of cereal before he could speak, he answered, "Yeah. I did."

"Well, I didn't. I was worried about you." She laid her hand on his arm. "I am worried about you."

Jason laid his spoon down and reached for his coffee. "Don't be. It's under control."

Rachael touched his hand. "Did you decide to tell her how you feel?"

Jason wiped his mouth with his napkin. "No."

She squeezed his hand. "But Jason, you have too."

"It's under control." He took another bite of cereal.

She squeezed his hand again. "Meaning…"

"Meaning it's under control."

Rachael let go of his hand, sat back in her chair with her arms folded, and looked at him. Jason stopped eating. "What?"

"I don't believe how pig-headed you are."

"I'm not being pig-headed. I'm trying to be submissive to the Lord."

Rachael moved up in her chair. "Look, Jason, I know that you are committed to doing God's will, but it's obvious to me that you two should be together. Maybe you should consider that it is God's will that you should be together."

"Rachael, it's in God's hands. I put it in God's hands. It's under His control."

"Have you prayed about telling her how you feel?"

Providencia   *Deborah A. Hodge*

Jason pushed his plate away. "Not exactly."

Rachael stared at him. "Why not?"

"Because she's engaged."

"She might not be if you tell her how you feel."

"I'm not that kind of guy. I don't poach on another man's territory."

"I told you that I'm not sure she is his territory now."

Jason looked her directly in the eyes. "If that's true she'll have to tell me that."

Rachael huffed. "I can't believe you are being so stubborn."

With that, Rachael shut up and nodded toward Luz, who was coming toward them. Jason turned his head to see Luz rushing over. She had a look of deep distress on her face. Katty and Roy followed her.

Luz grabbed Jason's arm as she protested. "Jason. Roy, and Katty say that I am to go with Roy today. I want to be on your team."

Jason responded diplomatically. "Roy has heard what a good translator you are, and he wants the opportunity to work with you."

His diplomatic tact did not work. Luz pouted. "But I like translating for you."

Katty intervened. "But I need to talk with Jason about trip matters. Therefore, I need to be his translator today."

Luz reluctantly nodded. She took Jason by the hand and squeezed as she agreed. "Okay, I will see you at lunch."

Jason smiled awkwardly. "Sure."

Roy took over. "Luz, I'd like to go over some phrases with you."

Luz agreed, and she let go of Jason's hand. "Okay."

Roy pointed to a table across the way. "Why don't we go over there and practice?"

Once they were out of earshot, Katty said, "I am glad Sarah talked with you about Luz."

Chapter 13

Jason's head darted in her direction. "How'd you know about that?"

"Roy saw her talking to you last night and told me when we were going over assignments for today. I was relieved. I should have spoken to you about it. Luz has had a crush on you from the first day. She has been constantly talking about you."

Jason's face revealed his surprise. "Really?"

"Yes. I'm sorry, I should have spoken to you myself. All of the translators noticed how she tried to monopolize your attention. I think her brother knew, too. That's why he was so mad at you."

Jason rubbed his face, closed his eyes and shook his head. "That's what Sarah said, but I had no idea."

Katty nodded. "I know. You're a wonderful Christian man. I can't blame her for falling in love with you. I could fall in love with you, too."

Jason's eyes popped wide.

Katty laughed. "I said could, not that I would. Besides, I'm only messing with you; I'm trying to lighten the moment."

Jason let out a deep breath, "Shoo. I'm not sure I can stand any more complications in my life right now."

Katty smiled. "It's okay boss. I'm here to help, not to complicate."

Jason rubbed his face again. "Thanks, help is what I need. Luz is set for today. What do we do about tomorrow?"

"No worries. I'll take care of it."

With pursed lips and a look of uncertainty, Jason responded, "I hope you can. I never meant for any of this to happen."

"I know," Katty said, "you're a good man."

"A foolish man."

"I don't think so. A foolish man would not be so concerned."

"Thanks, Katty."

"I am sure I can come up with a way to give you and Luz space. You're leaving in a few days. She'll come to her senses."

Providencia   *Deborah A. Hodge*

"But, I made promises to her about going to school in the United States, and I'd like to keep them."

"I know, and I think if we put some space between you and Luz that she will get over her infatuation with you, and keeping the promises will be much easier then."

"Sounds like a plan. Thanks for running interference for me."

"No problem. Glad to help."

The morning evangelizing progressed without a hitch. As the teams trekked back to the buses for lunch, Jason wondered what would happen with Luz. He soon had his answer. Roy's team had arrived before his team. When Luz saw Jason's team coming, she quickly made her way toward Jason.

She took his hand playfully and asked, "Hola, how did your morning go?"

Jason answered uncomfortably. "It went well, very well. We had twelve people accept the Lord."

Luz smiled. "We had fourteen."

Roy walked up and put his arm around Luz. "Luz is a fantastic translator."

Luz gave a broad, toothy smile. "Thanks Señor Roy, but I only translate what you tell me."

Roy tightened his arm around her shoulder. "Oh, I think you did more than that."

Luz continued to smile. "God gets the glory, and Sarah and Jason. I learned from them."

"Maybe, but some of what you did cannot be taught."

"Gracias," Luz said, as she blushed and brushed her hair from her eyes.

"I am very glad you are my translator today."

Luz smiled again. "Muchas gracias."

Jason added his appraisal. "I told you she was great."

Chapter 13

Roy gave Jason a wink and a nod. "Yeah, and you've been keeping her all to yourself."

Catching on, Jason tilted his head and pursed his lips. "Sorry."

Luz was persuaded of her excellence as a translator and the reason for her separation from Jason. Jason was relieved. Roy grinned and started toward the sack lunches. The teams devoured their lunches and everyone returned to spreading the gospel among the villagers.

Attendance at the night service highlighted the authenticity of the conversions of the day. The people came in droves and brought friends and relatives with them. Jason preached that night. The only member of the team missing was Sarah. She had called late in the afternoon to say that Rio was improving but wanted her to stay with him. She asked permission to return the next day. Jason agreed.

Back at the seminary, during the team's time of sharing and worship, Luz again attached herself to Jason. Things seemed fine until Katty suggested that Luz translate for Cannon's team the next day. She was not happy.

"But I want to translate for Jason again. There are only four days left before he returns to United States."

Katty spoke up. "You are right. There are four days left. You still have time to translate for Jason."

"But," Luz remonstrated.

"Luz, don't be selfish," Katty said.

Luz stood erect as her eyes flashed disbelief. "I do not mean to be selfish."

"Then be a member of the team. Share your skills with others," Katty chastised.

Luz dropped her head and reluctantly agreed. "Okay."

Luz was not very talkative at breakfast the next morning. She ate her food while intermittently glancing in Jason's direction. He was sitting with Katty, Rachael and Roy. Luz pushed her plate back, folded her arms, and watched as Jason and the others laughed as they glanced in

Chapter 14

her direction. She fumed at the possibility that they might be talking about her. However, she kept her distance.

When Roy announced that the teams should load the buses, still fuming, she walked slowly to the bus. Her body language and countenance shouted her discontent. She spoke to no one during the drive. She mulled over Katty's speech about not being selfish and being a team member and the possibility that Jason and the others had been talking about her at breakfast. She allowed herself to pout over being misunderstood. Anger seethed just under the surface. She was alone with her thoughts until Cannon slid into the seat beside her.

"I am so glad that you are translating for my team today."

Caught off guard, Luz responded, "Really?"

"You bet. I've heard what a good job you do. I don't want to miss out on the 'Luz experience.'"

Luz blushed. "Thank you, Señor Cannon."

"Cannon, just call me Cannon."

"Okay, Cannon. Thank you."

Once they arrived at their destination, Luz translated faithfully and reliably, though not completely whole-heartedly, for Cannon's team. Even so, the Lord blessed their efforts and five people gave their lives to Jesus.

When Sarah arrived during lunch, Rachael corralled her in an effort to nudge her toward Jason and to apprise her of the Luz situation.

"Glad to have you back. How is the little boy?"

Sarah smiled. "Thanks, he's much better."

Rachael handed Sarah a lunch. "That's great. Here you go."

"Thank you, but I had a late breakfast. Christian and I stopped on the way here."

"Christian seems like a very nice guy."

Sarah nodded. "He is."

"That makes you a very lucky woman." Rachael took a bite of her sandwich as she gauged Sarah's reaction to her comment.

Sarah did not respond immediately. She seemed to be chewing on Rachael's comment. Rachael gave her a moment before she put down her sandwich and continued. "I wish I had a guy like Christian."

"Huh?" Sarah looked confused.

"Lost in your thoughts?" Rachael inquired.

Embarrassed, Sarah answered, "Sorry, what were you saying?"

"I said I wish that I had a guy like Christian."

Sarah's expression changed and she began to probe. "I thought you had a guy."

"Me!" Surprise flooded Rachael's tone. "Whatever gave you that idea?"

"I've noticed your jealousy concerning Luz."

"Oh, you mean Jason."

Sarah looked her straight in the eye and nodded. "Yeah, I do."

Rachael bowed her head slightly and gave a little sigh. "Yeah well that's a one-sided proposition."

"Really," Sarah said.

Rachael nodded. "Yeah, Jason's not into me. He's in love with someone else."

Sarah's mouth flew open. She swallowed and echoed with surprise, "Someone else."

Rachael pursed her lips and nodded.

Sarah frowned as she considered the possibilities. "Who is she?"

"You need to ask Jason about that. By the way, I saw you talking to him last night."

Sarah answered quickly. "I was talking to him about Luz. I decided someone needed to make sure he realized what was going on."

"Yeah, he did, and you must have been able to get through to him

Chapter 14

because Luz has been translating for other people for the last couple of days."

"Wow," Sarah said as she sat up straight. "That's great."

Rachael returned to her sandwich. "It is, but she hasn't been too happy about it."

"How's Jason been with the situation?"

Swallowing a bite of sandwich, Rachael answered, "Embarrassed and worried. Why don't you talk to him?"

With a furrowed brow, Sarah breathed deeply. "Maybe I'll talk to Luz first."

Rachael nodded and Sarah rose to venture a conversation with Luz.

Luz was sitting by Carly, one of the translators about her age.

"Hola, amigas."

"Hola, Sarah," they both answered.

"Excuse me," Carly said, "I must speak to Señor Roy before we head back out."

After Carly had departed, Sarah smiled and began, "I hear that you have been doing a wonderful job."

Luz smiled a half-smile. "Gracias. It is because of you and Jason."

"That's not what I hear. Roy and Cannon have bragged that you have a gift for evangelism."

"I hope that is true. I want to tell everyone about my Jesus."

Sarah smiled as she touched Luz's arm. "And you're doing great at it."

"Gracias, Sarah."

"So which team will you be with tomorrow?"

Sarah empathized as Luz bit her lip and tears formed in her eyes.

Luz sniffed and answered, "I had wanted to translate for Jason's team, but Roy and Katty have assigned me to Señor Collin's team."

Providencia   *Deborah A. Hodge*

"I'm sure that you will enjoy working with Collin's team. They are very nice people."

Luz wiped her eyes. "Maybe, but Jason leaves in two days."

Luz's words jarred Sarah. Luz was right. Jason would be gone in two days and things had not been resolved between them. Sarah was sure that she was still in love with him, but evidently he was in love with someone else. She had received a surprise from God all right, but not the one she had hoped. What was she going to do? *Please God, help me.* Her time of reflection caused a lull in the conversation. The lull gave Luz an opportunity to plead for advice.

"Sarah, will you talk to Katty and persuade her to let me work with Jason until he leaves?"

Sarah's brow furrowed and eyes narrowed. "I'm not sure I should do that. Katty is in charge."

Luz pleaded, "Sí, I know, but please try. She will listen to you."

"I don't know, Luz. I don't think I should interfere."

Luz was not pleased. "I thought that you were my friend."

Sarah's face contorted. "I am your friend, but I am also just a translator like you. Katty is our boss."

Luz reluctantly acquiesced. "Okay, I will translate for Collin tomorrow, but it must be Jason next day."

Once again Luz translated well, but half-heartedly. The joy had disappeared from her face. Things came to a climax with Luz that night when Katty assigned her to work with Thomas' team the next day.

Disappointment flooded Luz's face. "But this is the last day of evangelism. Please let me work with Jason's team."

"Mika is working with Jason's team. She has not had the opportunity to do so."

Luz saw Jason walk into the cafeteria and yelled for him. "Jason!"

The tone of her voice caused Jason to stop immediately to ascertain what was going on. Luz bolted in his direction.

Chapter 14

"Jason, please tell Katty to let me translate for you tomorrow."

Luz's sudden arrival caused Jason to back up. "What's going on?"

Katty caught up with Luz. "Luz is upset because I asked her to work with Thomas tomorrow."

Luz grabbed his arm and pleaded. "Please tell her to let me work with you."

Looking down at Luz, Jason said, "Luz, Katty is in charge of translators. I don't think I should interfere."

Luz's eyes popped in protest. She huffed loudly, "But you are in charge of her."

Jason was speechless. He stood with eyes wide and mouth open.

Realizing that he was not going to intervene with Katty, Luz stood straight with folded arms and an angry look on her face. "I thought that you would understand, and that you would be on my side. I thought you would want to be with me the last day of evangelism."

Jason looked at Katty. His eyes darted back and forth, as he tried to find the right response. "Luz ..."

Luz cut him off. "I thought you liked me."

He tried to calm her down. "I do like you. You're a nice young woman."

Luz stepped back and launched into a tirade: "My brother was right. You are the one with the smooth tongue. You make promises that you do not intend to keep."

"That's not true."

Luz cocked her head and stared. "I think it is true. I think I have been deceived."

"Luz, it's not true. I haven't deceived you. I intend to keep my promises."

Luz shook her head. "I do not think so. I think you are trying to get rid of me. That's why I am not translating for you anymore."

Luz glared at Katty as she intervened. "That is not true. I make the assignments, not Jason."

Providencia   *Deborah A. Hodge*

Luz brushed the hair from her face, cocked her head, folded her arms and said, "But, you work for him. He could intervene if he wished."

Luz watched as Jason stood speechless. She frowned and continued her harangue. "I think you are trying to get rid of me. If you want me to go, I will go."

"You are being silly," Katty protested.

With arms stilled folded, Luz stared at Jason for a response to Katty's statement. "If what I say is not so, Jason would say it, but he only stands there."

Jason stammered a response. "I don't know what to say. I am not deceiving you."

"Then tell Katty that I must translate for you tomorrow."

Jason looked at Katty to help him craft a response. His actions ignited Luz. "I see that I am not being silly and I quit. I am going home." She began her very angry exit.

Luz seethed as Jason stammered, "But…"

Katty jumped in. "No, Luz, don't quit. Stay for the remainder of the trip."

Luz stopped, turned and stood staring at Jason. She waited for his apologetic response. He stared back, not knowing how to defuse the situation. Impatiently, Luz whirled around and stomped toward the door.

"Wait Luz," Katty called.

Luz's head spun around and she shouted over her shoulder. "I don't think so!" She hurried out the door.

Jason stood frozen in disbelief. "Wow, I didn't see that coming."

Katty nodded. "Nor did I, but I guess that solves the problem with Luz."

"I'm not sure it does. She was so angry. I don't think she'll ever let me explain," Jason said. He sighed. "I never wanted her to be hurt or have her miss out on an opportunity to go to school in the United States."

Chapter 14

"Give it time," Katty said. "Maybe you can still help her."

"I hope so."

No one moved as each one watched Luz walk out the door. As she exited, their focus turned to Jason and Katty. Sarah, Rachael and Roy rushed over.

"What happened?" Roy asked.

Katty explained, "She was upset because I didn't assign her to work with Jason tomorrow."

"Oh," Roy said, with a nod.

Jason shook his head in frustration. "She accused me of deceiving her and trying to get rid of her so I could renege on the promises I made."

Sarah touched his arm. "Look, I'm sorry. I might have been able to prevent this. She wanted me to talk to Katty. If I had, maybe we could have worked things out."

"I don't think so," Katty said. "She was determined to be with Jason tomorrow. I don't think that she would have accepted anything but that."

"So maybe we should have allowed her to," Jason responded.

Rachael chimed in, "I don't think so. I think this had to happen sooner or later."

"I think Rachael's right," Roy said.

"Maybe, but I'm sorry it happened this way," Jason sighed.

"I'm sure everything will be okay. Just give Luz a chance to cool off and think about it," Sarah suggested.

"That's what I suggested," Katty said.

"I hope you're both right," Jason responded.

"Why don't we pray about it?" Roy suggested, as he held out his hand. Everyone nodded. Sarah's position in the group next to Jason meant that she would hold his hand while they prayed. As she slipped her hand in his, she glanced at his face. His face revealed confliction. She offered a sympathetic look. He sighed and gripped her hand. Roy voiced the prayer as they committed the situation to God.

Providencia　　　　　　　　　　　　　　　　　*Deborah A. Hodge*

The fruits of the next day's evangelism efforts were beyond anyone's expectations. Paired with church members, ten teams trekked through one of the poorest areas of the southern outskirts of Quito. The people were friendly and receptive to the gospel. Some were already Christians and went along with the team members to tell neighbors about Jesus. When time came for the groups to return to the buses at the end of the day, they reported more than two hundred professions of faith.

Everyone was ecstatic. Singing and joy filled the buses as they made their way back to the seminary. Traffic was extremely heavy. Consequently, the drive back to the seminary took longer than usual. Once back at the seminary, the teams only had an hour before they were to leave for the final revival services at the cooperating churches. The teams hurriedly consumed dinner.

For the final revival services, the leaders combined the teams into four groups. Once everyone was ready, they boarded the buses that would drop them off at cooperating churches. Katty went with Roy's group. Sarah went with Thomas' team. Mika went with Jason's, and Marlene went with Cannon's group.

Once the services were ended, the bus that had delivered Thomas' and Jason's groups began the journey to retrieve Jason's group from Vida Nueva. Jason's group was waiting for pick-up, and everyone filed onto the bus, everyone but Jason.

Thomas intercepted Mika as she entered the bus. "Where's Dr. Jason?"

Mika's face revealed her concern. "He's on an errand. He said he would meet us back at the seminary later."

Sarah frowned. "What kind of errand?"

Chapter 15

"A man came with a message from Luz's parents. They asked to meet with Jason," Mika answered.

A look of concern flooded Sarah's face. "He went alone?"

Mika nodded. "I tried to get him not to go alone. I offered to go with him, but he said no."

Trying to get things straight, Sarah repeated, "You said a man came with a message."

Mika nodded again. "Yes."

Sarah touched Mika's arm. "Was it Luz's brother?"

"I don't think so, but I am not sure. I didn't see him yesterday."

Carly interrupted. "It was not Luz's brother."

"Are you sure?" Sarah asked.

"Sí, I saw him myself. It was not Luz's brother."

Worry took over and Sarah's eyes mirrored her concern. Thomas tried to console her. "I'm sure it's okay. Dr. Jason's a smart man."

Sarah nodded in agreement. "He is, but Jason's out of his element in Ecuador. He shouldn't have gone alone."

Thomas agreed, "Yeah, he and Dr. Roy told us not to go anywhere alone. I guess he broke his own rule."

Sarah sighed, "Uh-huh he did, and I hope it doesn't get him into trouble."

"Sarah, I'm sorry. I should have insisted that Jason take me with him," Mika said.

Sarah forced a smile. "It wouldn't have done any good. Jason has a mind of his own."

The drive back to the seminary took twenty-five minutes.

Roy was waiting for the bus. Mika and Sarah jumped off. Sarah quickly walked toward Roy and reported. "Jason may be in trouble."

"What?" Roy shouted with concern. "How's that?"

Mika had hurried to find Katty, and Katty quickly joined Sarah and Roy.

"Mika told me about Jason. I'm afraid he might be in real trouble."

"Someone please explain to me what's happened?" Roy pleaded.

Mika explained. "A man was waiting for Jason after the service tonight. The man presented him with a note from Luz's parents. They asked Jason to come to their house to meet with them."

"So what's the problem?"

Katty spoke very plain. "The man was probably not from Luz's parents."

Roy's eyes popped. "Oh!"

Sarah sighed. "He probably was from Luz's brother, and he doesn't like Jason at all."

Roy considered the possibility. "So he might want to harm Jason."

Katty once again spoke plainly. "I'm afraid he might want to kidnap Jason."

"Kidnap him," Roy echoed.

Chapter 16

Katty nodded. "Sí, I really think that Eduardo is connected with FARC and they frequently kidnap people for ransom."

"Do you really think that might be a possibility?"

"I'm not sure what's going on here, but it could be a possibility."

Ascertaining the severity of the situation, Roy excused himself. "I'll be right back. I need to go get things started."

Ringing her hands, Mika asked, "Do you think we might be over-reacting? He could be with Luz's parents, couldn't he?"

Katty and Sarah's faces answered her question. She closed her eyes and prayed.

Roy returned quickly. He had put Cannon in charge of the sharing and worship time so that he, Katty and Sarah could focus on the situation with Jason.

"What do we do?" Roy asked.

"We need to talk to Luz and her parents to be positively sure that he is not there," Sarah answered.

Katty answered quickly. "I will call Luz. I have her number." She retrieved her cell phone from her pocket, checked her address book and pushed the buttons. Finally, Luz answered.

"Luz, this is Katty Gándara. Is Jason with you or your parents?"

"He isn't. Did your parents send a message asking to see him?" Katty covered her phone with her hand. "Luz doesn't think, but she is asking her parents." Luz was quickly back. "They didn't."

Katty shook her head. Her eyes revealed her increased concern, which was contagious. Roy stood shaking his head in disbelief. Sarah couldn't wrap her head around the situation. Katty began again, "Is your brother with you? ... He isn't. Do you know where he is?" Katty shook her head again. Things were getting worse. "Thank you, Luz." Katty nodded. "Yes, Jason is missing. He left Vida Nueva tonight thinking that your parents had asked to meet with him." She nodded again. "There was a messenger who claimed to have a note from your parents." She nodded as she continued to listen to Luz. "Yes, he was alone." Katty nodded. "Yes, he said the note was from your parents. That's why I think your brother may be involved" ... Katty shook her head. "No, not yet, we will wait a short time to see if he returns; if not we will contact the authori-

Providencia   *Deborah A. Hodge*

ties." She nodded again. "Yes, I'll let you know. Goodbye." She closed her cell phone. "I am very worried. The messenger lied to Jason, and there is almost no doubt that Luz's brother is involved. I'm not sure we shouldn't just go to the police now."

Sarah bit her lip and swallowed hard. "I think you're right."

Roy agreed as he began pacing back and forth. "I can't believe this is happening. Jason should have known better than to go off with that guy."

Sarah nodded. "But, you know how upset he was about the whole thing with Luz. I'm sure he thought he might be able to fix things."

"Maybe it was Luz's brother who sent the note and maybe he just wants to talk to Señor Jason," Mika said.

Katty's tone was not hopeful. "Maybe, but this is not good. Jason doesn't know Spanish or Quito."

Sarah took a deep breath and let it out slowly. "I'm afraid not knowing Spanish and Quito might be the least of Jason's problems."

Everyone nodded in agreement.

"Let's pray," Roy suggested. Everyone joined hands and prayed for Jason's safe and swift return.

Rachael walked up just as Roy was saying amen. "I don't mean to intrude, but I was wondering if any of you knows where Jason is. I haven't been able to find him since we returned."

Sarah shot a distressed looked at Roy and Katty.

"I'll tell her," Roy said.

Rachael suddenly realized from the look on their faces that something was wrong. The realization colored her tone. "Tell me what?"

Roy paused as he searched for words. The pause frightened her even more.

"Tell me what's wrong. Where's Jason?"

Roy's eyes narrowed and his jaw clenched before he spoke. "Jason's disappeared."

"What?" she gasped. "How?"

Chapter 16

"He received a message supposedly from Luz's parents asking to see him, and he went."

"Alone!" Rachael blurted.

Roy nodded. "Alone."

Rachael put her hand over her mouth. "Why would he do that?"

"You know Jason. He's a fixer. He probably thought he could fix things with Luz."

Rachael bit her fingernail. "Yeah, probably, and he thinks he is impervious to danger."

Sarah spoke up. "I'm not sure he thinks about himself at all."

"You seem to know him well," Roy observed.

Rachael let the cat out of the bag. "They went to school together in Kansas."

Roy cocked his head. "I thought you two had a history."

"Really," Sarah said.

"I thought so too," Katty admitted.

Embarrassed at her transparency and not liking the direction of the conversation, Sarah took a deep breath, let it out, and pointed to her watch. "Jason's been gone almost two hours. I don't think we should wait any longer. We need to contact the authorities."

Katty agreed. "You are right." Katty was about to make the call when Luz rushed up.

"Has Jason returned?" she asked.

Everyone shook his or her head.

Luz began to cry. "I believe it was my brother who sent the message."

Everyone's eyes widened.

"Why do you think that?" Katty asked.

"Because he knew I was very upset, and he blamed Jason for it. He said that he would see to it that Jason couldn't hurt me anymore."

"What?" Rachael shouted.

Luz nodded as tears streamed down her face. "And, Katty I think you were right. I think my brother is with FARC."

Sarah's hand flew to her mouth as she gasped at the seriousness of it all. Tears pooled and ran from the corners of her eyes. *This is very, very bad.*

Katty grimaced. "We must call the authorities." She grabbed her phone and pushed the appropriate buttons. While Katty was talking with the authorities, Thomas joined the group.

"Dr. Roy, have you heard anything from Dr. Jason?"

"No, Thomas. We haven't."

"Everyone's spooked by this whole thing. Cannon wanted to ask you what he should tell them."

"I'll talk to them. I'll be there in just a minute."

Thomas nodded. "Okay Doc." He began his return to the cafeteria.

Roy waited for Katty to finish her conversation. "The authorities are beginning to investigate."

"The group is getting antsy. I need to explain to them what is going on," Roy said.

"And, the group needs to pray," Rachael said.

"Yes, that would be very good," Katty agreed. Wiping tears, Sarah agreed.

"Sarah and I will go to meet with the authorities while the group prays," Katty said.

Sarah sniffed to clear her nose. "And, we'll take Mika with us. She's the only person who saw the man who brought the message to Jason."

Roy reluctantly agreed. "Okay, I'll take care of things here. You two take care of things there."

"I will go, too," Luz said.

With her hands on her hips, Katty agreed. "If you think your brother really did do this, I think that would be a good thing."

Chapter 16

Sadly Luz replied, "I don't want to think so, but I do."

"Okay, let's go," Katty said, pointing to a small blue car. "My car is over here."

"Good luck," Roy said, as he and Rachael walked toward the cafeteria.

"Good luck to you, and pray hard," Katty replied, as she, Sarah, Mika and Luz got in and drove away.

Arriving at the central police station, the women met with the chief. When it became clear that there was a possibility of FARC's involvement, the assistant chief had phoned the chief, and he was waiting to question Luz about her brother and Mika about the man who delivered the message. A sketch artist created a sketch of Luz's brother, and using Mika's description, he produced a picture of the messenger. Sarah provided a photo of Jason. All police personnel received copies of the pictures as they canvassed the area where Jason disappeared.

After the interviews, the chief invited the women to wait in his office. He was in and out and on the phone the whole time. The women were confident that he and the police were trying their best to locate Jason.

"I am so very sorry," Luz sobbed, "This entirely my fault."

Sarah gently touched her arm. "You shouldn't blame yourself."

"Why not blame myself? It might not have happened if I hadn't been such a…"

"Baby," Mika interrupted.

Luz dropped her head, "Yeah, baby."

Sarah and Katty shot a disappointed glance in Mika's direction. Mika relented.

"I'm sorry. I shouldn't have called you a baby. I know you really like Jason."

Luz looked up through tear-filled eyes. "Yeah, I do. I should know my brother would over- react."

"How could you have known that?" Sarah asked.

Chapter 17

Wiping tears, Luz confessed, "He has always over-reacted. He's always treated me like baby." She sniffed to clear her nose and frowned as she realized, "I guess it's because I've always acted like baby."

Sarah tried to smile. "Well, tonight you acted very grown up. It took a great deal of courage to admit that your brother might have done this and to give the police a picture of him."

"I wish Jason liked me as I like him."

Sarah pointed out, "Luz, Jason never intended to hurt you. He was just being nice. He's nice to everyone."

Mika added, "He didn't realize how you felt about him."

"I know, but it did hurt," Luz sobbed. "That's why I was so angry. But I didn't want anything to happen to Jason. My brother misunderstood."

"Your brother did not like Jason from the start."

Katty jumped in, "I think your brother did not like Jason because Eduardo is connected with FARC." Katty's brow furrowed, "I am afraid that if the police do not find him soon, Jason is in very big trouble."

The words cut like a dagger. Trying to conceal her distress, Sarah looked away. "Maybe the police will find him."

"Maybe," Katty hoped aloud.

Four hours passed before any information came. Katty used her cell phone to keep Roy and the others apprised of what was happening. All of the women prayed.

At three-thirty in the morning an officer knocked on the door, poked his head in and asked to speak with the chief. The chief motioned him over. They spoke discreetly. The chief excused himself and left the room.

Katty and Sarah gave each other a hopeful glance. "Wonder what is going on?" Luz asked.

"Maybe good news," Mika answered.

"I hope so," Katty said.

"Do you think they have found him?" Luz asked.

"That would be very good news," Sarah answered.

Providencia   Deborah A. Hodge

"Very good," Katty agreed.

As the chief re-entered the room, he took a seat close to the women.

"My officers have found the messenger."

"Really," Sarah gasped. "Did they find Dr. Parks?"

"No, I am afraid not, but he did confirm that it was Señorita Gutierrez's brother who sent the message."

Luz covered her mouth as she blurted, "Oh no!"

"Your brother paid the messenger and forced Dr. Parks at gunpoint into a truck. The messenger was so frightened that he ran away. After a couple of hours, he decided that he should confess to us what had happened. Señorita Gutierrez, does your brother own a truck?"

"I don't know. I have never seen one."

"The messenger said another man was driving the truck. He knows that it was white, but he has no idea what type of truck."

Tears had begun to flow freely from Sarah's eyes as she heard the words "forced at gunpoint." She tried to get a hold of her emotions as she asked, "What will you do?"

The chief tried to reassure the four women. "We are searching for the truck, but there are many white trucks in Quito."

"Sí," Katty agreed.

"They may have already taken Dr. Parks away from the city. If so, it will be much more difficult to find him, but we will not give up. I also think it is time to contact the American authorities," the chief said.

Katty and Sarah nodded.

"It is four o'clock in the morning, but I will help you make the call if you wish."

"Yes, please," Sarah said. The chief rose and escorted Sarah toward the desk. He dialed the number, spoke a few words in Spanish, and handed the phone to her.

"Hello, I am Sarah Barnes, an American, and need to speak with Ambassador Hodges. Yes, I need to report," her voice cracked, "an abduction." She nodded. "Ambassador Hodges I am sorry to call this early, but

Chapter 17

I need to report the abduction of an American ... Yes, Dr. Jason Parks. He's a professor at Midwestern Seminary in Kansas City, Kansas. He was leading a mission team." She sniffed as she listened to the official on the other end. "Yes, ma'am, he was taken tonight at gunpoint. The chief will give you the details. Yes, the group is at the Nazarene Seminary. Thank you ma'am, we'll be expecting you." Sarah handed the phone to the chief.

As the chief filled in the details for the ambassador, Sarah related what Ambassador Hodges had told her.

"She promised that she would work with the Ecuadorian authorities to do all that she could to find Jason. She also said that she would meet with the team at the seminary tomorrow at ten."

"Good," Katty said.

The confirmation that her brother had taken Jason shook Luz. While Sarah was talking to the chief, she had called her parents to inform them. Finishing the conversation with her parents, Luz began to sob uncontrollably. Katty and Mika had tried unsuccessfully to comfort her.

As Sarah walked over, Luz blubbered, "I am so sorry that my brother did this. I am so sorry."

Sarah sat beside her and put her arm around her. "It's not your fault, Luz."

"But it is. I knew my brother did not like Jason and I spoke ill of him because I was mad at him. I'm sure it made my brother furious enough to do this."

Sarah shook her slightly. "Listen Luz, no matter how much we may dislike someone that does not give us the right to seek to harm that person. You are not responsible for your brother's actions. He is."

"Sarah's right," Katty said.

Mika and the chief nodded in agreement. "Sí, she is right."

Sarah stood up. "We had better get back to the seminary. Thank you, Chief, for all that you have done and are doing."

"You are very welcome. I am sorry that this thing has happened in my country."

"Muchas gracias, señor," the other women said, as they rose to leave.

Providencia   *Deborah A. Hodge*

"De nada! I will have my officers accompany you to the seminary. We will keep an eye on the rest of you."

"Thank you, Chief," Sarah said.

The return to the seminary was a very somber trip. All four women knew the situation was grave. None of them voiced their fears. The police escort behind them underscored the gravity.

Back at the seminary Roy, Rachael, Cannon, Collin and Thomas met them as Katty parked. Everyone else was asleep.

"What's up?" Roy asked.

Katty and Sarah explained while Luz sobbed and apologized. Everyone tried to reassure Luz that she was not to blame, but she would not be comforted. Finally, Rachael took possession of her and ushered her to her room to go to bed. Everyone except Roy, Sarah and Katty followed suit. Roy noticed the police presence.

"We have company, huh?"

"The chief has positioned his men to protect us should FARC want to kidnap someone else," Sarah explained.

"Does he really think they might?" Roy asked.

Katty nodded. "That is how they make their money. They kidnap people and hold them for ransom."

Roy frowned with puzzlement. "They're expecting to get ransom for Jason."

Sarah folded her arms and sighed. "I'm not sure that it's as simple as that. I'm afraid Luz's brother is out for revenge against Jason."

Katty's eyes narrowed. "Let's hope it is simply ransom. If so they will keep him safe."

Tears streamed from Sarah's eyes. She hoped that it was a ransom thing, but she was afraid it wasn't. She prayed that Jason was safe.

Roy and Katty recognized her distress. Katty hugged her. "He'll be all right."

Roy patted Sarah's back. "Sure he will. We've been praying, remember?"

Chapter 17

Sarah sniffed and swallowed tears. "I hope you're right."

Katty looked at her watch. "What time did Ambassador Hodges say she was coming in the morning?"

Sarah continued to sniff and wipe tears. "Around ten."

Roy's eyes widened. "The ambassador is coming to the seminary."

Katty nodded. "Yes, she's coming to give us an update."

Roy blew out a deep breath. "We'd better get to bed. That's only about five hours away."

They headed to their rooms. Sleep came easy for none of them. Each tossed and turned, as the what-ifs robbed them of their rest. Sarah fell asleep praying. "Please, Father, take care of him. Please bring him safely back to us. Your word says that You are our refuge and strength and a very present help in trouble."

The other team members had gone to bed at one and awakened by seven. Roy had decided the night before that the teams would not go out evangelizing that day. Instead, they would stay and pray for Jason's safe return.

Rachael, Katty and Luz got up about eight and left Sarah sleeping. When she did awake and looked at her watch, she panicked. It was nine-thirty, almost time for the ambassador's arrival. She hurried to shower, dress and get to the cafeteria to meet with the ambassador.

Walking toward the cafeteria, she saw Katty and Roy coming to meet her. "Is there something wrong?"

Roy spoke first. "The ambassador's office called and said that she would be an hour late."

A look of worry took control of Sarah's face. "Did she say why?"

Katty added, "We think maybe there will be an update on Jason."

Sarah pondered what that might mean. Seeing the look on her face, Roy said, "Maybe it will be good news."

Sarah prayed he was right. "We surely need good news, don't we?"

However, it was not good news. When Ambassador Hodges arrived, she introduced herself and apologized for being late, and explained, "I am very sorry to keep you waiting, but I wanted to verify the latest information that I have received. A couple of hours ago, the authorities received a tip from an informant. He reported that he had encountered a truck fitting the description of the one driven by the abductors near the small town of Lago Agrio. When the driver left the truck for a few minutes, the informant caught a glimpse of a man tied and unconscious. The informant notified the authorities immediately, and they tried to inter-

Chapter 18

cept the truck. However, by the time they arrived, the truck had crossed border into Colombia at the jungle village of Puerto Nuevo."

Roy grasped at a straw of doubt. "Are you sure that the unconscious man was Dr. Parks?"

The ambassador nodded slowly. "I'm afraid so. The informant had the photos, and was sure of what he had seen."

Shaken by the news, Sarah asked, "So Jason's in Colombia. What do we do now?"

The ambassador answered frankly, "I've contacted my counterpart in Colombia and he has informed the Colombian authorities. They have promised to do all that they can to find and free Dr. Parks."

Everyone nodded.

"Dr. White, have you contacted your seminary back home and Dr. Parks' family?"

"I've contacted the seminary. They contacted his family."

"Good because the news media have picked up the story. It will be reported around the world."

Katty interjected, "FARC likes publicity. Maybe that will ensure Jason's safety." Roy nodded.

Sarah prayed silently. *Please God, keep Him safe.*

The ambassador spoke frankly again. "I hope that's right, but they're more interested in ransom than publicity. Can your seminary afford to pay ransom, Dr. White?"

Roy shook his head. "I doubt it."

The ambassador posed another alternative. "Can his family?"

"I'm sure they can't," Roy answered.

The ambassador's face filled with concern. It f illed the room, but Sarah's concern quickly morphed into terror.

"What if no one can pay ransom?" Sarah asked.

Once again, the ambassador was very straightforward. "I do not know, Miss Barnes. They usually only abduct high-value targets, those for which they are sure they can receive a large ransom."

Katty tried to offer a glimmer of hope. "They have been known to hold their captives for months or even years hoping to receive a ransom."

Seeing the distress on the faces, the ambassador played along. "You're right, Miss Gándara. That does happen."

Roy and Sarah weren't convinced that she was being straightforward this time, only kind.

The ambassador addressed the immediate and more difficult subject. "I believe your group is scheduled to leave Ecuador at 10 p.m. tonight."

"Yes, we are," Roy responded.

"I will make the arrangements for your exit to be safe, smooth and quick."

"Thank you that would be very much appreciated," Roy said. "But if you could help me, I'd like to make arrangements to stay until there is some word from the kidnappers or Jason is found and returned."

The ambassador nodded. "Of course, but you must understand that this is going to be a long drawn-out process. It will probably take months to reconcile."

That statement startled Sarah. *Months, oh Father please don't let it take months.*

Roy nodded. "Yes, but if my seminary agrees I'd like to stay for a while."

"Of course," the ambassador said, "I'll be glad to help you."

The ringing of Roy's cell phone interrupted the conversation. "Excuse me please; it's the president of my seminary."

"Of course," the ambassador replied.

Roy moved to where he could have more privacy, and Sarah began her own personal inquiry.

"Has anything like this happened before?" she asked.

"Yes," the ambassador answered, "a few times, but usually only with high-value targets, such as company executives."

Chapter 18

Katty agreed, "Not with American missionaries."

Sarah's eyes and face flashed terror again. "So this is really, really not good."

The ambassador touched her shoulder. "Groups like FARC are unpredictable. Maybe they've changed their way of doing things."

"And maybe this is not about ransom," Sarah said.

"What do you mean?" the ambassador asked.

"One of the men who abducted Dr. Parks is brother to one of our translators. There was a misunderstanding and she became very upset. It may be that her brother wanted revenge against Dr. Parks," Katty explained.

The ambassador's face mirrored new concern. "I hope that is not so."

"Yes, we hope not also," Katty replied.

Tears streaming from her eyes, Sarah struggled to control herself as she asked, "How do you think that would change Jason's prospects?"

"I don't know, Miss Barnes."

Roy returned from his phone call. "President Roberts says the seminary trustees are doing what they can to prepare for a ransom demand. He's contacted the board of trustees, but he isn't very hopeful that a large sum of money can be raised."

Sarah broke down. Katty and Roy quickly put their arms around her. The ambassador watched and tried to think of a comforting yet truthful thing to say. "Let's hope they won't ask for much."

Roy and Katty nodded. The ambassador's aide approached and whispered something in her ear.

"I'm sorry, but I must return to my office and take care of another matter. Is there anything else I can do for you before I go?"

Roy stuck out his hand. "No, we appreciate all that you have done. You have been very kind and helpful."

Returning Roy's gesture, the ambassador said, "That's one of my responsibilities. I am glad to help. Someone from my office will contact you about the airport arrangements and arrangements for you to stay."

Providencia   *Deborah A. Hodge*

"Thank you, Ambassador," Roy replied.

"You are welcome." The ambassador retrieved her hand, walked to the car, waved, got in and drove away.

Roy turned toward the women as he collected his thoughts. "I guess it's time to go tell the others what's going on."

Sarah was still a mess.

"I'll stay with Sarah while you tell the others," Katty suggested.

Roy nodded and walked slowly to the cafeteria to inform the others. Collin, Cannon, Thomas and Rachael met him halfway. He stopped briefly, said a few words, and proceeded toward the cafeteria.

Collin and the others stood dumbfounded for a moment before the men slowly followed Roy to the cafeteria.

Sarah was still sobbing and Katty was still holding her as she cried. Rachael put her arm around her and tried to bring fresh comfort. "He'll be okay, Sarah. God will take care of him."

"I hope so," Sarah uttered in a whisper.

"Sarah, you know God is in control. He works all things together for good, and He will this time. It is His promise," Katty chimed in.

"I know," Sarah said. "I'm just afraid of what they will do to him."

"Only what God will allow," Katty pointed out.

Rachael nodded as she stroked Sarah's hair. "We can trust God," Rachael said.

A car entered the gate, and two men and a woman got out, interrupting their effort at consolation.

Katty and Rachael immediately recognized Christian but were not sure who the other two were.

The trio walked quickly toward Sarah.

The woman's voice tenderly called, "Sarah."

Sarah raised her head immediately, "Mother!" Seeing those accompanying her, Sarah continued, "Dad! Christian! Her mother and dad quickly traded places with Katty and Rachael, while Christian stood

Chapter 18

looking on, as did Katty and Rachael.

"FARC has Jason," Sarah blubbered.

"We know, honey," her mom said.

Her dad added, "Christian saw it on the news very early this morning. He called us, and we all came as quickly as we could."

Sarah raised her head and thanked Christian. Her swollen and bloodshot eyes betrayed the length and depth of her despair. Christian graciously accepted her appreciation, though Katty, Rachael and Sarah's parents could see his distress at Sarah's depth of concern for Jason.

"Any news?" Sarah's father inquired.

"They have taken him to Colombia," Katty answered.

Christian cleared his throat and responded, "That is not good."

"No it's not," her father agreed.

"I am sorry, my Sarah," Christian said, and turned toward Rachael and Katty, "I am sorry."

"Thank you," was their collective response.

"I am sure everything that can be done is being done," Sarah's father said.

"Yes, sir," Katty answered. "The ambassador was here this morning. She has contacted Michael McKinnie, the American ambassador in Colombia, and he informed the Colombian authorities."

"Has there been a ransom demand?"

"No, Mr. Barnes, not yet," Katty answered.

"You must be Katty Gándara," Sarah's mother observed. "Sarah speaks highly of you. I can see why."

"Thank you, Mrs. Barnes." Katty motioned toward Rachael. "And this is Rachael. She works at the seminary with Dr. Jason and Dr. Roy."

Mrs. Barnes smiled. "It's nice to meet you, Rachael. Sarah has told us about you also."

"It's nice to meet you all, but I'm sorry it's under these conditions,"

Providencia   *Deborah A. Hodge*

Rachael answered.

"As are we," Mrs. Barnes said.

With her parents still embracing her, Sarah was trying to collect herself, while wiping tears and trying to clear her nose and throat. Finally able to speak clearly, Sarah added, "The group is leaving at ten tonight, but Roy is staying," she directed her next statement to Christian. "I'd like to stay too, if it's all right."

Christian shifted his feet. It was apparent that his heart was not in what he was about to say. He clenched his teeth momentarily before he answered, "Of course."

Sarah's eyes flashed her appreciation as she reached out for him. "Thanks."

Christian nodded uncomfortably as he moved toward her. He held out his hand and Sarah clasped it in hers.

"Christian has to get back to the hospital tonight, but we are going to stay with you," her dad said.

Sarah agreed with a brief smile. "Thanks, that would be great."

Chapter 18

Providencia   *Deborah A. Hodge*

The remainder of the day was very solemn. Members of the group fretted, prayed for Jason's safety, and reluctantly prepared to leave Ecuador without him.

Sarah's parents had prevailed upon her to lie down and rest. She submitted, and she did manage to sleep for a few hours. Sarah awoke to see that Rachael was keeping vigil over her while she slept.

"Where are my parents?"

Rachael lowered the book she had been reading. "They're at the cafeteria with Roy."

"And Christian?"

"He's there, too."

Still lying in bed, Sarah rubbed her face and put her arm across her forehead. "Any more news about Jason?"

Rachael shook her head as she answered, "No."

Sarah rubbed her face again and let out a deep sigh.

Rachael scooted toward the edge of her bed. "Sarah, I'm sorry about all of this."

"Thanks, it's hard on all of us."

Rachael nodded and paused. She took a breath and began again. "Yeah, it is, but I know about you and Jason."

Sarah became very still and quiet for a moment. "What do you mean, you know about me and Jason?"

"I know that you two were engaged, and that he still loves you."

Sarah was silent as she wiped the tears that were dripping from the corners of her eyes.

Rachael ventured another observation. "I believe that you still love him, too."

Except for intermittent sniffs and the swallowing of tears, Sarah didn't respond. Rachael left it alone and continued her book. Sarah finally responded, "How did you find out about us?"

"I wormed it out of Jason. I knew there was someone from his past that he had never been able to forget. He had told me about a ghost that haunted him."

Sarah swallowed and responded. "Ghost."

Rachael nodded. "That's what he called you."

Sarah sniffed and laid her arm on her forehead as she stared at the bunk above her. "That's not very flattering."

"It's more flattering than you know. He meant that you were the girl that he couldn't get over."

Sarah raised her head slightly. "How can you be sure that he meant me?"

"His reactions when he saw you the first night at the airport made me suspect something, watching you two together intensified my suspicions, and the night of your conversation with him about Luz, and Christian's arrival, confirmed every suspicion. I pushed Jason to talk about it. He confessed all."

Sarah took a deep breath. "Even that he still loved me."

"Even that," Rachael answered very forthrightly.

Sarah covered her face with her hands and shook her head. "Everything is such a mess."

"I agree."

Sarah dropped her hands to her chest. "Did he tell you why we called our engagement off?"

"He did."

Sarah raised her head and looked at Rachael. "Then you know that nothing has changed."

Rachael scooted to the edge of the bed, walked over, and sat on the bunk beside Sarah's bed.

"Something has changed. After four years, you're both in the same hemisphere, and he loves you and you love him."

Sarah closed her eyes, put her arm back across her forehead and shook her head in frustration.

"Look, Sarah. He came as the leader of the group by default because the professor who was supposed to be in charge had to have surgery and couldn't come. He's here because of God's providence, and by God's providence a translator dropped out and you took her place. Don't you see God is up to something?"

Sarah pondered a moment, and admitted, "I don't know. I just know God's in control."

"That's what I'm saying. He's in control and He's always at work in our lives even though we don't realize it. Circumstances have conspired to get you and Jason in the same place after four years. That's the providence of God. It's His working behind the scenes to accomplish His purpose in your life and Jason's."

Sarah dropped her arm to her side. "Maybe, but there's something else I don't understand."

"What?"

"I know that you have feelings for Jason, too. Why are you telling me all of this?"

"I told you. My feelings for Jason are totally one-sided. When I figured out about you two, and he told me that he still loved you, I knew I didn't have a chance with him, and besides, I think you two are meant to be together."

Rachael's statement shocked Sarah, but she could tell by Rachael's expression and the tone of her voice that she was being painfully honest. Sarah's face flashed a true apology. "I'm sorry."

Rachael shrugged her shoulders. "Actually, I was glad to find out about you. After trying to get Jason's attention for more than a year, I was beginning to think something must be wrong with me."

Chapter 19

The door creaked as someone opened it slightly. Mrs. Barnes was checking on Sarah.

"How are you, honey?"

"I'm okay."

Her mom walked over and sat down on her bed. "Are you sure?"

Sarah glanced at Rachael. Rachael dismissed herself. "Well, I'll let you two have some privacy."

Sarah smiled. "Thanks Rachael. You're a good friend."

Rachael returned her smile. Her mom smiled and mouthed, "thank you," in Rachael's direction. Once Rachael had exited, Sarah's mom tried again. "How are you really?"

Sarah shook her head in perplexity. "Everything is such a mess."

Her mother let her talk. "Rachael told me that Jason is still in love with me. I am positive that Christian knows that I still love Jason. Terrorists have abducted Jason and have taken him to Colombia, and I have no idea how they're treating him or if I'll ever see him again. Things can't get much worse."

Her mom patted her leg. "Honey, things may get worse, but God is in control and we can trust Him."

Sadness and frustration captured Sarah. "That's what everyone keeps saying, and I know it's true, but I'm having such a difficult time leaving everything in His hands."

Her mom patted her again. "I know, sweetie. I've been there."

"You have?"

"Of course I have. I struggled with trusting God when we almost lost you, and when Mama Carrie had cancer. I had to deal with real feelings and chose to put things in God's control repeatedly, and it wasn't easy. It's a choice we make, honey, not a feeling."

"Mom, my feelings are so raw and mixed up."

Her mother gave her another tender pat. "I know."

Sarah breathed a deep sigh. "What time is it?"

Providencia   *Deborah A. Hodge*

"It's about three."

"Where is everyone?"

"Gathered in the cafeteria mostly."

"How is everyone?"

"They're all worried about Jason and don't want to leave without him. But Roy and Katty are trying to keep their spirits up and point them to God."

"Yeah, they're good people, good Christian leaders."

Her mother smiled. "Yes, they are. I like them very much."

Sarah cleared her throat. "Where's Christian?"

"He's waiting in the cafeteria, but I'm sure he needs to be getting back to the hospital."

Sarah sighed and ran her fingers through her hair. "I guess I need to go talk to him, but I don't know what to say."

"Did you tell Jason how you feel about him?"

Sarah shook her head. "No! I've been so conflicted, and he was so busy." Sarah's voice trembled, "Besides, I didn't know he still loved me."

Cate touched her daughter's arm. "That's a shame, honey."

An ache flooded Sarah's eyes and spilled onto her face. "Mom, what's changed for Jason and me? And what about Christian?"

Cate took a deep breath before she answered. "Let's take Christian first. It's not fair for you to marry him if you are in love with another man, especially if he knows." Sarah nodded, wiping tears again. "And now let's talk about Jason. Sarah, God's gone out of His way to bring you two together again after four years. I think He's trying to show both of you something if you'll let Him."

Sarah protested in frustration. "What, Mom? What's God trying to show us, especially by allowing Jason to be kidnapped?"

"That I cannot answer, but you can trust Him and allow His providence to work."

"That's what Rachael said."

Chapter 19

"Smart girl."

Still wiping tears, Sarah asked for advice. "Mom, what do I tell Christian?"

"The truth, you tell him the truth."

Sarah knew she must tell the truth, but she also knew that actually doing it would not be easy.

Her mother immediately recognized Sarah's trepidation and suggested that they pray.

"Sarah, honey, why don't we pray about everything before you see Christian?"

Sarah nodded quickly. Her mother held out her hand. Sarah clasped it gratefully and squeezed tightly. They smiled at each other, and her mother began, "Father, You know exactly what is going on, and why You have allowed it. I know Sarah wants to follow You with all of her heart. Please help her know how to do that at this time in her life. Please give her the strength and wisdom to say exactly what she needs to say to Christian, and please help her to trust You completely with Jason, Christian, and the working out of Your will. Father, please take care of Jason wherever he is." Sarah trembled at the mention of Jason. Her mother patted the hand she clasped, and continued, "Father, You have promised to work all things together for good for Your children, and we claim that promise knowing that You are a faithful and true God. I put my daughter, Jason, Christian, and everything into Your hands right now. In Jesus' name, I pray."

Sarah sniffed and stumbled her way through a prayer of submission and trust. "Oh, Father," she sighed. "Please help me. I do want to follow You with all my heart, but I can't see clearly. I don't know what You are asking me to trust You to do, so I am just going to choose to trust You to do whatever is best. Father, Christian is a good man, a godly man, and I don't want to hurt him." She paused to sob, collected herself as best as she could, and began again. "Father, help me to be compassionate, but honest. Please help me to tell Christian the truth in a way that will honor and glorify You." She wiped her face and nose with her hand, sniffed and finished, "In Jesus' name, I pray."

Her mother squeezed her hand, gathered her into her arms and whispered, "It'll be all right, Baby Girl." Sarah nodded, surrendering to her mother's hug. Finally, Sarah raised her head and prepared herself for what she must do.

Providencia   *Deborah A. Hodge*

As she entered the cafeteria, Sarah spied Christian seated with her dad, Roy, Rachael and Katty. She paused to gather herself, took a deep breath, and plunged ahead.

As she walked over, everyone inquired as to how she was feeling.

"Much better. I guess I needed some rest."

"We all did," Katty replied, "I slept for a couple of hours myself."

Sarah nodded. "Any news?"

Roy shook his head. Sarah turned her full attention to Christian. "Thanks for staying. I'm sure you were needed at the hospital."

"Dr. Ramirez is covering, but I do need to get back soon."

Sarah nodded slightly. "I know. How about taking a walk with me before you go?"

Christian paused a moment, then nodded. Sarah held out her hand. He rose, took it and they walked toward the door.

Ambling along, holding Christian's hand, Sarah couldn't bring herself to broach the subject. Christian recognized her pain, and reluctantly came to her rescue. He stopped, turned toward her and asked, "You still love him very much, don't you?"

Sarah stopped, dropped her head, and nodded.

"I thought so."

Sarah looked up, her eyes filled with tears, and her face with sadness. "Sorry," she said as she swallowed hard.

Sarah sighed as she watched Christian choke back his emotions. "Don't be sorry. I know this is difficult for you."

Tears trickled from Sarah's eyes. "I'm sorry for not telling you about Jason when you asked me to marry you."

"I'm not sure you could have. I think you buried your feelings for him. Remember, your parents and I made you come to Quito to face him."

Sarah's tears flowed freely. "I'm so sorry. I never meant for this to happen."

Christian took her hand. "You don't have to be sorry. I knew this could happen, but I needed to know."

Sarah clasped his hand. "You're such a good man."

"Not that good, just realistic."

Sarah squeezed his hand, looked into his eyes and said, "I'm sorry for what has happened to us."

Christian gently touched her face and replied, "All that has happened to us, my Sarah, is that two very good friends have found out that they should not marry."

Sarah's eyes glistened with tears. Christian cupped her face in his hands. "Don't cry. It's better to know now than after we have made a mistake."

Sarah put her hands over his hands, sighed and said, "I'm so sorry."

"Do not be sorry. We cannot control matters of the heart when they're tied to God's providence."

Sarah nodded and repeated. "God's providence, everyone keeps talking about God's providence, but I don't understand what He's doing in my life."

"Sí, God's providence is sometimes difficult to understand, but He is trustworthy. He makes no mistakes."

"I know that He is trustworthy, but none of what's going on makes any sense."

Christian brushed a tear from her face and smiled. "It does to God."

Providencia　　　　　　　　　　　　　　　　　*Deborah A. Hodge*

Sarah raised her left hand, slowly slid Christian's ring off her finger, and handed it to him.

Genuine warmth and affection filled his eyes, as he nodded, took it and dropped it into his pocket.

"I guess I'll be getting back to the hospital. I'll check on you later today."

Sarah nodded as he took her hand, and bent down to look her in the eyes. I'll be praying for Jason … and you."

Tears were visible again, as Sarah tried to smile. "Thanks."

Christian nodded, smiled, and reminded her, "Put it all in God's hands. Trust His providence." She closed her eyes, sighed, swallowed tears, and nodded.

"Goodbye, Sarah," he said in a low but resolute tone. She opened her eyes. With tears streaming down her cheeks, she sniffed, wiped tears and reciprocated, "Bye." He let go of her hand and walked away.

Sarah sighed deeply, brushed the remaining tears from eyes, looked up to the heavens, and said, "God everything's up to You. I put it all in Your hands and trust Your providence." She cleared her nose, swallowed hard and walked toward the cafeteria.

Her mother met her. "Is everything okay?"

Sarah bit her bottom lip as she nodded slightly. Her mother brushed her hair from her eyes and hugged her.

"So Christian didn't take it well?"

Tears filled her eyes and she frowned as she answered, "I think he took it too well."

"What do you mean?"

Sarah corralled the tears that fell from her eyes and landed on her lips. "You were right. He told me, before I told him."

Her mom smoothed Sarah's hair. "It's been pretty evident since the day you heard Jason was coming to Ecuador."

"Mom I never meant to hurt Christian."

Her mother said, "He knows that. We all know that."

Chapter 20

Sarah wiped her face, brushed her hair over her shoulder, and cleared her nose again.

Her mother glanced at her. "Are you ready to go back in?"

She shook her head. "I think I'll stay outside for a while."

"Okay, Baby Girl. I'll see you in a bit."

Sarah made her way to the steps of the seminary offices and sat down. The offices were far enough from the cafeteria and the rooms that she could sit in undisturbed silence. She grabbed her knees and cradled her head on top of them. Her head was pounding from all of the tears and tension. She refused to allow herself to think about the things she had given to God, and actually dropped off to sleep.

Her father's voice interrupted her nap as he touched her shoulder. "Sarah, Ambassador Hodges is here."

At first, Sarah thought she was dreaming and didn't open her eyes, until she heard him speak again. "Sarah, honey, she has news about Jason."

Sarah raised her head and peeked to make sure she wasn't dreaming. Seeing her father, she rubbed her eyes as she asked, "Did you say there is news about Jason?"

Her father nodded. "Yes, honey, Ambassador Hodges is here."

"It must be something serious if she's come in person."

Her father took her hand and helped her up. "Let's not jump to conclusions. Let's go see."

They hurried to the cafeteria. They entered just as the ambassador was handing something to Roy. Sarah and her dad joined the group surrounding Roy.

Shock filled Roy's face. He nodded briskly. "Yes, that's Jason."

"Thank you Dr. White. We needed to be sure."

The group strained to get a peek at the picture. Everyone gasped as each one saw a bruised, dirty Jason, tied to a pole that restrained his arms behind his neck.

"Ambassador McKinnie's office received this picture and a ransom

---

Providencia   *Deborah A. Hodge*

demand about two hours ago."

Roy shuffled his feet. "What kind of demand did they make?"

"They asked for one million dollars."

Everyone's mouth flew open. Sarah looked at her parents in disbelief as she repeated, "One million dollars."

"That's crazy. There's no way the seminary or anyone else can raise a million dollars," Roy said.

Ambassador Hodges tried to put it into perspective. "This is a beginning figure. We can negotiate."

David, Sarah's dad, voiced everyone's question. "Do you think they will negotiate?"

"Yes, I do."

Roy inquired further. "Do you think he'll be okay until we get things worked out?"

"I think he will. He's their golden goose. If they harm him, he goes down in value."

"Or maybe they think the seminary will pay quicker if they threaten harm," Rachael said.

"No one can be sure what his captors will do, but I can assure you that Ambassador McKinnie and I will do everything we can to facilitate his release as quickly as possible. Maybe I can even help with the ransom if that becomes necessary."

Everyone breathed a sigh of relief at Ambassador Hodges' generous offer. Roy took the lead in expressing their collective gratitude. "Thank you, Ambassador, for all that you have done and for what you are doing. If you will excuse me, I'll contact President Roberts and let him know what's going on." Roy reached for his cell and began to move away.

Ambassador Hodges stopped him. "Dr. White, I've made arrangements with Ambassador McKinnie for you to stay in Bogotá until we reach a resolution regarding Dr. Parks if you'd like, or you are welcome to stay in Quito. It's your choice."

Roy thought for a minute. "Thank you, Ambassador, I'll let you know by the end of the day."

Chapter 20

The ambassador nodded. "That'll be fine. I'll meet your group at the airport tonight to say a final farewell."

"That is very gracious of you, thank you."

Ambassador Hodges smiled. "Nonsense, it's part of my job. I'll see you around ten tonight."

Roy returned her smile. "Yes ma'am."

Sarah had been able to see the picture while the group had jockeyed for a glimpse of it. Once they had moved away, she had moved in for a closer look. Her heart skipped a beat as she saw him bruised, bleeding and tied to the pole. She stood stunned and quiet. Her mind raced with the possibilities of what might be happening to him at that very moment. The picture made her face the reality that she really might never see him alive again, and it rocked her. She struggled with the truth that God was in control of the situation no matter what the captors were doing or planned to do. She knew the truth of God's faithfulness and dependability, but counting on that in this situation was difficult for her. She knew this was a test of her faith. She prayed silently, "God help me. I've put Jason in Your hands, but my emotions are running wild. Help me to pay more attention to You than them."

Her mom recognized the signs of her panic and quietly ushered her away from the group so she could talk with her.

Once out of earshot, her mother tried to comfort her. "Sarah, I know it looks bad."

Sarah's eyes darted directly toward her mother's. "It looks very bad."

Her mother nodded. "I know, but God is in control."

Sadness took control of Sarah's eyes. "I know, Mom, but it's still bad."

"It is, but trust Him anyway. God knows what He's doing."

Sarah dropped her head. "Yeah, but I wish I knew, too."

Her mother put her arm around her and drew her close. "I know, but that's where faith comes in. We trust Him when we don't understand. Sometimes God tests our faith with trials. Remember faith that can't be tested can't be trusted."

"I know, but it's hard."

Providencia   Deborah A. Hodge

Her mother nodded sympathetically. "I know it is, but that's how He has called us to live."

Sarah's body shook as she sobbed. "Mom, what if I never see Jason again?"

Cate took Sarah in her arms and hugged her tightly. "Put it in God's hands, and trust Him to work."

Sarah closed her eyes as she said, "I feel so helpless."

"I know; put even that in God's hands. Trust Him for the strength to get you through."

"What if things don't work out the way I want?"

"There is no guarantee that things will work out the way you want, but that's when we trust God's wisdom. We choose to trust Him over and over again, even if our emotions and circumstance push us to panic and question His wisdom."

Providencia Deborah A. Hodge

Jason was having a similar crisis of faith. When he woke from his unconsciousness, he had no idea where he was. It took him a moment to realize that Eduardo and his amigo were not solely responsible for his captivity. Many people surrounded him, and he very shortly found out that they were as unfriendly toward him as Eduardo and the other man had been.

When they realized that Jason was awake, they taunted him as Eduardo had. Though he did not understand their words, he knew they were disparaging. He was in a bad situation and he knew it. He was grateful that God's Spirit brought Scriptures to help him cope. As his captors mocked him, his mind replayed the verses he had memorized.

"When I am afraid, I put my trust in you. In God, whose word I praise-- in God I trust and am not afraid. What can mere mortals do to me? (Psalm 56:3 and 4) Surely God is my salvation; I will trust and not be afraid. The LORD, the LORD himself, is my strength and my defense. (Isaiah 12:2) God is our refuge and strength, an ever-present help in trouble. (Psalm 46:1)"

A big man who seemed to be the leader yelled something in Spanish. Silence took over as two men picked Jason up by his arms, which Eduardo had tied behind his back. Once they had him up on his knees, they untied his hands and two other men placed a pole on his neck and shoulders. The two who had untied his hands retied them to the pole. After the two men had secured Jason to the pole, a man stepped forward with a camera and snapped a picture. The flash momentarily blinded Jason. Before he regained his sight, the two men who had secured him to the pole grabbed the pole and dragged him into a nearby hut.

Overbalanced by the pole, Jason fell with a thud onto the dirt floor, and the two men took up guard stations at the front door of the hut. Shortly after Jason was moved into the hut, Eduardo paid him a visit.

Chapter 21

Eduardo entered and laughed at the sight of Jason crumpled on the dirt floor. Jason stared at his jubilation. Eduardo fell to his knees, bent down and got in his face. "Now gringo, your seminary and you will pay for the way you treated my sister."

"What do you mean 'the way I treated your sister'?"

Eduardo pointed his finger. "You led her to believe that you had feelings for her."

Bewilderment covered Jason's face. "I did not."

Eduardo gritted his teeth and spewed angrily, "You led her to believe that you would take her to America."

Jason shook his head. "I did not. I promised to see if I could help her go to school in America, not take her to America."

Eduardo bounced back on his heels and yelled. "You lie."

Trying to support himself on his right elbow, Jason protested, "I am not lying."

Eduardo lunged toward Jason and pushed him backward onto the dirt floor, and with his left hand against Jason's chest he raised his right fist. "Are you calling my sister a liar?"

The pole penned Jason's arms, but he tried to draw his head back. "No, she's simply mistaken."

Eduardo thrust his fist forward. Jason squirmed and tried to use his legs to counter. Eduardo dodged his attempts and jumped to his feet. He grabbed at the pole, jerked Jason upward and then threw him to the ground, moving quickly to put his right foot on Jason's chest. He pressed so hard that Jason struggled to breathe. "You are the one who is mistaken if you think you can lead my sister on without consequences."

Struggling to take in enough air to speak, Jason worked to get out the words, "I never led your sister on."

Eduardo moved his foot toward Jason's throat. "You are like your country; you think you can do as you will without consequences. I will teach you that is not so." Eduardo tried to make good on his threat as he raised his foot to stomp Jason's throat. Jason used his feet to move himself out of the way. Persisting in his efforts to crush Jason's windpipe, Eduardo kept lunging at him.

Providencia *Deborah A. Hodge*

He would have succeeded if the leader of the group had not intervened. He grabbed Eduardo and pulled him backward just as he was about to hit his mark.

"¡Levántate!" he yelled.

Eduardo reluctantly obeyed.

"Fuera," the leader demanded.

Eduardo complied and left. The leader helped Jason up. "Are you all right, Dr. Parks?"

"Yes, thank you, but how do you know my name?"

"I know everything about you."

"Really?"

"You are Dr. Jason Parks, a professor from a seminary in America. You brought a group of students to Ecuador and tonight you were to return to America. Am I correct?"

"Yes."

"I also know that Eduardo hates you."

Jason stretched his neck from side to side. "I know that, too."

The leader smiled. "I'm sure that you do, but you do not know that he brought you to us at my suggestion."

"And you are?"

The leader proclaimed proudly. "I am Calberto, leader of these freedom fighters."

"Freedom fighters?"

"You may know us as FARC."

Jason frowned. "I think I have heard of you."

Calberto trumpeted, "We are one group of many here in Colombia. We fight oppression of the poor and helpless."

Jason frowned again. "So what am I doing here?"

Calberto grinned. "You will help us continue our fight."

Jason's face revealed his confusion. "How?"

"We must have money to fund our operations, and your seminary must pay us for your freedom."

Jason's eyes widened at the statement. "My seminary doesn't *have* money to pay for my freedom."

Calberto smiled. "I do not believe you, Señor Doctor. We have asked a million dollars for your return."

Jason's mouth flew open. "A million dollars! There's no way."

Calberto's eyes narrowed and his face took on a menacing look. "They will pay to get you back. If not today, tomorrow or whenever, we can wait, but not for always."

With that, he turned and walked out the door. Jason tried to grapple with questions that rattled around in his brain. *What in the world is going on? Why, God, have you allowed this? I don't understand. Help me to understand. I am totally helpless. God, You're my only hope. Help me, please. What must everyone be thinking? What must Sarah be thinking? God help them and me. I know nothing happens that You don't allow, and whatever You allow You have a purpose for allowing. Please help me see what You're trying to teach me here, and what You want me to do in this situation. Father, help me. I have no idea what's going to happen, but I know that I can trust You. Help me to live in Your strength and wisdom, and help me to be a witness to my captors. Help me to return good for evil."*

Eduardo interrupted Jason's prayer. "Now Professor Gringo, we will see how important and indispensable you are. We have asked a million dollars for your safe return."

"You will be sadly disappointed. My seminary does not have a million dollars."

Eduardo folded his arms. "You had better hope they do."

"Hoping won't make it so. I know they don't have it."

With a devilish grin on his face, Eduardo trumpeted, "Then you will die."

"Then I will die."

Providencia　　　　　　　　　　　　　　　　　　*Deborah A. Hodge*

Eduardo tilted his head and gave him a puzzled look. Finally, with a smirk he said, "You gringos make no sense. I know you do not want to die."

Jason smiled slightly. "You're right. I don't want to die, but if I do, I'm ready to die."

Eduardo shook his head in disbelief. "You are loco."

Jason shrugged the best he could while tied to a pole. "Not loco, just prepared to die."

Eduardo uttered a huff. "No one is prepared to die."

"People who have placed their faith in Jesus Christ are prepared to die."

"So now you will be a martyr."

"I'm no martyr. I'm just a follower of Jesus."

Eduardo yelled. "You are a liar. Jesus would have never treated my sister the way you did."

Jason shook his head in protest. "I did not mistreat your sister!"

Eduardo stood tall with folded arms, gritted teeth and a clenched jaw. "We have been through this before. You put big ideas in a poor Ecuadorian girl's head. A fancy American professor having his fun with a pretty Ecuadorian girl. It was a game for you."

Jason looked him straight in the eyes. "I wasn't playing games. I meant every word I said to your sister."

Eduardo stared back in anger. "And that is why she came home crying."

"She came home crying because she misunderstood why she was reassigned as an interpreter."

"What did she misunderstand? She told me that you did not want to be around her, that you had lied to her."

Jason shook his head. "It wasn't that. Your sister thought she was in love with me. I didn't want her to get hurt. I didn't want to encourage her, so I distanced myself from her."

Eduardo exploded in fury. "You are a liar. You made my sister cry.

Chapter 21

You hurt her. You took advantage of her and then threw her away."

"I did not throw her away and I did not mean to hurt her."

"Now you will see what it is like to be hurt." Eduardo lunged at Jason and lashed out with his fists. He caught Jason full on the jaw with a left hook, and then a right.

Jason was helpless as Eduardo's fists slammed his head to the left and then the right. He tried to dodge as Eduardo tried for a second round. One of the guards who realized what was going on stormed in and grabbed Eduardo.

"Déjale," the guard said. Eduardo did not stop.

The guard ran out the door.

Suddenly Calberto entered with the guard and yelled, "Déjale."

Eduardo submitted to Calberto's command and left.

Seeing blood trickling from Jason's mouth and nose, Calberto pushed Eduardo and yelled, "Idiota."

"This gringo disrespected my sister," Eduardo yelled back.

Calberto slapped Eduardo across the mouth. "I said no more beating. He is valuable to us."

Eduardo rubbed his mouth. "He said that his seminary could not pay."

"They all say that," Calberto replied.

"But I think he speaks the truth."

Calberto shot a threatening look toward Jason and laughed. "If he speaks the truth, he will have a short life."

"He says he is ready to die."

Calberto laughed again. "If no money comes, we will see."

Eduardo and the guard joined Calberto in laughter. Calberto grabbed a handful of Jason's hair and pulled him toward the light so he could take a good look at his face. "Not too much damage. Eduardo, you hit like a girl."

Providencia   *Deborah A. Hodge*

Eduardo shook his head and smiled. "I don't think the gringo would agree."

Jason did not agree, and even though his face hurt, he stared in silence.

Calberto smiled. "You stare, but you do not answer. You are much of a man or you are a coward. I do not know which, but we shall see."

Jason continued to stare. Calberto laughed and walked out, followed by Eduardo and the guard.

Chapter 21

Providencia   Deborah A. Hodge

Jason was left alone in the hut. Blood dripped from his nose and mouth, and his hands were of no use to wipe them. He used his tongue to corral the blood so he could spit it out. *Lord, please don't let there be many more days like this. Keep me safe, O God, for in You I take refuge.*

Jason fell asleep praying for strength and wisdom in the situation. *Lord, Your word says that "You are my refuge and strength, a very present help in trouble. You promised never to leave me or forsake me. What time I am afraid I will trust in you. I can do all things through Christ who is my strength."*

At sunrise the rebel camp was astir with preparations to move. Guards rousted Jason from sleep and released him from the post. They tied his arms behind his back and dragged him to a waiting truck, shoving him in the back where two other guards were waiting.

Jason heard enough Spanish and broken English to ascertain that the rebel location had been compromised, so they were moving. Even though he could see the landscape from the back of the truck, he had no idea where they were. All he knew was that they traveled for hours before they stopped.

At the new site Jason was unloaded, allowed to eat, and put in a new hut. However, this time he was chained to a pole in the center of the hut. He had enough chain length to lie down to sleep and to relieve himself in a dignified manner.

The hut had no electricity, no running water, and no furniture except for a bed frame with a straw mattress. A window allowed sunlight and moonlight to shine in. The guards delivered food and water to Jason twice daily and emptied the pail that served as a chamber pot once daily. This would be his home for the next several months.

The days passed slowly. Jason noted the days the best he could by marking the pole that restrained him. He tried to recite enough Scriptures daily to keep him fed spiritually. His mind reflected on Joseph in Genesis, and God's faithfulness during times of mistreatment. He remembered how God had worked through the adverse circumstances to prepare Joseph for the fulfillment of God's promises to him. He repeated to himself Genesis 50:20, "You meant it for evil, but God meant it for good." Jason knew God had not changed. He hung on to that truth and prayed day by day for God's sustaining grace. Praying Scriptures was part of his daily routine. He prayed Psalm 31:15 "My times are in your hands; deliver me from my enemies and from those who persecute me." Psalm 18:2 "The Lord is my rock, my fortress, my deliverer; my God is my rock, in whom I take refuge." These two verses helped to sustain him.

While the days turned into weeks and the weeks into months, Jason watched the activities of the camp through the window and gleaned enough information to know that negotiations for the ransom were ongoing. He was surprised but glad that his captors were still negotiating with the seminary. He couldn't believe his captors would wait so long for payment. He was convinced that the only reason they were willing to wait for payment was that God was answering his prayers. He knew God had blessed him by keeping him alive.

God had also blessed him with not seeing Eduardo for months, not since the day they left the first camp. Jason wondered whether Calberto had sent him on another mission or he was in Ecuador with Luz and their family or he was somewhere else. He wondered about what was happening at the seminary. Were they trying to raise the money to free him? Most of all, he wondered about Sarah and how she was being affected by all this. He had been gone for months. He wondered whether she married Christian. He wished he had told her that he loves her.

He once again mulled over the question of why. *Why, God, have you allowed this? I have been a captive for all of these months. None of what happened in the last months or the last four years, for that matter, makes any sense to me. The whole thing with Sarah and me four years ago, having to be team leader in the Ecuador mission trip and seeing Sarah again, loving Sarah more than ever, her being engaged to Christian, and me being kidnapped.* He asked again as he whispered in prayer. "God what are You trying to do? What are You trying to teach me? Please, whatever it is, help me see it." He quoted parts of Psalm 42 and Hebrews 13 to himself to bolster his resolve to trust God no matter what. "Why are you cast down, O my soul? Why are you so disturbed within me? Put your hope in God. For He has said I will never leave you or forsake you."

His puzzlement about Eduardo ended. He spied him as he made his entrance into the camp. He had learned some more Spanish while in

Providencia　　　　　　　　　　　　　　　　　　　　　*Deborah A. Hodge*

captivity and listened as fellow rebels greeted Eduardo. He understood enough to know that Eduardo had been in a village near Bogotá. Calberto had given him the task of bringing new recruits and supplies, and he was congratulating Eduardo on his success. He heard Eduardo say his name, and knew he was inquiring about the state of negotiations. He listened to the reply to Eduardo's inquiry and knew that ransom negotiations were ongoing and that Calberto had lowered the ransom demand. That tidbit of information ignited a slight hope within Jason that his release would be soon. He prayed that it would be so.

Later that afternoon, Eduardo burst into Jason's hut. "Hello, gringo. I hear that you are doing well. I wanted to see for myself." He eyed Jason. "I see that you are slimmer and trimmer. Now you know what my people go through under this repressive government. They, like you, have only enough food to survive."

Jason looked him directly in the eyes. "Thank you for your concern. Although I could use a shower, haircut and shave, I am fine."

Eduardo shook his head at Jason's audacity. "You are loco just as I said."

"Not loco, just not very presentable."

Eduardo stroked his mustache. "My friends tell me that you have been very well behaved."

Jason's eyes narrowed. "I'm not sure what you mean by that."

"I mean that my friends speak well of you, and how cordial you are to them. They are your captors, your enemies, but you treat them as if they are your friends. You must be loco."

A faint smile found its way to Jason's face. "I serve a Savior who tells me to treat well those who are my enemies or those who mistreat me and to pray for them."

"Sí, my friends said that you say that. That makes you idiota and loco. Enemies must be killed, not treated well."

With the faint smile still apparent, Jason shook his head. "That is not what Jesus says in the Bible, and I must follow Him as long as I live, and I must tell everyone who will listen that He loves them and died to save them. I cannot share that message if I mistreat others or kill my enemies."

Chapter 22

"You are muy loco. No one can live that way. You will see. Before we are through with you, you will hate us."

Jason again looked him straight in the eyes. "It's not going to happen."

Over the following weeks Eduardo and his friends, with Calberto's permission, tried to break his resolve. His tormentors laughed at his pain, hunger and thirst. He became an object of derision and sport. They deprived him of food and beat him. But Jason didn't change. By the grace of God, he was a steadfast witness whose behavior gave credibility to what he believed. Though cursed, he did not curse. Though bruised and beaten, he did not lash back. Though not taken care of as he had been, he prayed for his abusers as well as for his release.

The attempt to break his resolve lasted for two months and ended just as abruptly as it began. Eduardo disappeared again. Jason guessed that he was on another mission to resupply and recruit.

Any days free from abuse were a delicious relief to him. The guards once again were business-like instead of abusive. Once again, they provided two meals a day with water and the emptying of his chamber pot. Though he remained almost completely unwashed, long-haired and unshaven, he enjoyed relatively peaceful days and nights as the months continued to pass. He prayed daily, "To You I call, O Lord, my rock, do not turn a deaf ear to me. The troubles of my heart are enlarged, bring me out of my distresses. Lord, I don't know what You're doing, but I know You are at work. Please let me be released soon."

Providencia   *Deborah A. Hodge*

The months of his captivity crawled by for all those who waited for Jason. They were especially difficult for Sarah. Roy had stayed for a month after the team had gone home, but he had to return to the seminary even though the authorities had not found Jason.

Sarah had returned to the hospital at Otavalo and thrust herself into work, Scripture and prayer. This made the situation tolerable. However, fears, frets and anxieties haunted her during her down time, especially at night.

Nightmares invaded her dreams almost every night. She could see Jason in the distance. He was smiling, but as she headed toward him, a look of anguish would replace the smile. She could hear him call her name. She tried with all her might to reach him, but she couldn't. She watched in horror as he disappeared. She called his name, but no answer. This is when she usually woke.

Often she yelled so loudly while dreaming that she woke her parents, who had come to stay with her. Her mother and father would take turns trying to comfort her until she fell asleep again. It took months, but her parents' patient comfort and prayers helped in her determination to defuse and defeat the nightmares. God also used her parents and Christian to keep her on an even keel in her daily life. As she shared her discouragements, her parents reminded her of their experiences with the faithfulness of God. They urged her to cultivate her relationship with the Lord.

"Sarah, time reading the Scriptures will help you weather this crisis."

"I know you're right, Dad."

Her mother caressed her face. "Honey, God's word was an anchor for me when we almost lost you."

Sarah nodded. "And you didn't lose me. I don't know that I'm ever going to see Jason again."

"That may be true, but you do have the assurance that you can trust God no matter what."

Her dad added, "And Scripture gives you that assurance. Don't give in to your night terrors or daytime fears. Fill your mind with Scripture."

"Spend lots of time in prayer as you wrestle with your anxious emotion," her mom added.

"Okay," Sarah agreed.

Sarah found that they were right. Scripture and prayer connected her with God's faithfulness and she remembered that He was her refuge and strength. She slowly grew in the ability to stake her life and Jason's on His sovereign power and unchangeableness.

She was glad that God had used Christian also. He became an encourager and allowed her to vent.

"Sarah, you can share anything with me. I'll advise you the best I can and I'll pray with you."

"Thank you Christian. To have you as a friend is truly a blessing."

Even with all of this support, there were times when she had almost given up, and it was then that God in His grace gave her enough news to keep going. Two months after Jason's abduction, Sarah's phone rang.

"Hello."

"Sarah, I have news."

Sarah felt faint but mustered enough strength to ask, "Ambassador Hodges, is it good news or bad news?"

"I think it might be good news. An informant has reported to Ambassador McKinnie that people had seen a man fitting Jason's description riding in the back of a truck headed east. Even though the information was more than a month old, the Colombian authorities and Ambassador McKinnie were chasing down every possible lead."

"That is good news."

"It could be. Ambassador McKinnie was very hopeful. That's why I

Providencia   Deborah A. Hodge

called. But I want to add a note of caution. We won't know anything for sure until the information has been completely checked out."

Sarah swallowed hard. "When will that be?"

"There's no way to know for sure, but I wanted to keep you in the loop."

"I appreciate it."

"I'll call you when everything has been checked out."

"Thank you, Ambassador. Goodbye."

As she hung up the phone, she voiced a prayer of thanksgiving, "Thank you, Father, that he might be still alive. Please help him."

Three months later, right after church, the ambassador called again. "Sarah, we have new information. A villager in southern Colombia heard that rebels were holding an American in a village twenty miles to the east of his village. Authorities are checking out the tip. I'll let you know as soon as I know."

"And, you think it's Jason?"

"The information suggests that it could be him. I'll let you know more as soon as I know more."

"Thanks, Ambassador Hodges."

Sarah was cautiously optimistic. She quickly shared the news with Christian and her parents.

"Sarah, that's great," Christian said.

Sarah sighed as she nodded. "Yeah, maybe."

She was afraid to be too encouraged by the news. Her mother put her arm around her daughter and drew her close. "It's good news, honey."

Sarah's eyes narrowed and she bit her lip as she nodded again.

Her father tried to buoy her faith. "Sarah, it'll be all right."

She finally spoke in a low, hopeful tone. "I know, Daddy."

Chapter 23

Everyone tried to carry on normal activities as they waited with quiet trepidation for the ambassador's call. The trepidation turned into disappointment.

"Sarah, I'm sorry it wasn't Jason. It was an American oil worker who had been kidnapped a year ago by FARC."

Sarah listened with tears running down her cheeks. "Thank you for calling, Ambassador Hodges."

"I'll call again when I have more news. I'm sorry to have gotten your hopes up."

"I'm glad for the other man's family."

"Me too. Sarah, we'll get Jason back, too."

"I know; thank you, Ambassador."

"Goodbye."

Sarah wiped tears. "Goodbye."

As she hung up the phone, she shared the ambassador's news. "It wasn't Jason; instead it was an oil worker who had been held for a year. The ambassador said that she'd call when she had more news."

Her mother walked over and hugged her. Her father and Christian watched with empathy.

"If they've kept the oil worker alive for a year, Jason's okay too," her father said.

"I hope so," Sarah said in a whisper.

"Believe it," Christian replied with conviction.

"I'm trying to," Sarah answered.

"Let's pray about it," her dad suggested.

They sat down, joined hands and prayed. Her father voiced their prayer.

"Father, we thank you for your watchful care over the oil worker and that he was found and freed. We thank you for your sustaining grace and we pray that you will take care of Jason just as You took care of the other man. Father, You have been so good to help us get through these

---
Providencia   *Deborah A. Hodge*

last months. We pray that You will help us simply to trust You and Your providence. We know that You are working in ways that we cannot see. We thank you for that."

Her father's prayer boosted her spirits. She once again silently committed her life and Jason's to God. *God, I know that Your word testifies of Your concern for Your children and Your constant care. I trust You, Father, to take care of Jason, my family, Christian and me. I put it all in Your Hands and I am willing to wait for Your time and Your working things out the way You want. I choose to trust you and submit to You and Your will.*

The next day Rio came for his monthly check-up. "Nurse Sarah, are you all right?"

Sarah bent down to give him a hug. "I am. Why do you ask?"

He grabbed her face and looked into her eyes. "Your eyes say differently."

Sarah smiled, but her eyes did not. "You are a very bright young man."

"No, but I know you. Your eyes don't smile like they used to."

Sarah hugged him again. "I love you, Rio."

"I love you, too, Nurse Sarah. I want you to be happy again."

"Me too, Rio," Sarah said, as she straightened his collar and brushed his hair from his eyes.

"I am praying for you."

Sarah tried to smile through her eyes. "Thank you."

"I am praying for your friend Jason, too."

Sarah's face revealed her puzzlement. "How do you know about Jason?"

"I asked Dr. Christian why you were so sad. He told me."

"I see."

"I thought it was because Dr. Christian and you are no longer getting married. He told me it was because your friend Jason was in danger."

"Yes, my friend Jason is in danger. He was kidnapped by rebels from

Chapter 23

Colombia."

"Oh," Rio said, as his face flashed concern. "I am very sorry, Nurse Sarah."

"Thank you, Rio. He is in God's hands."

Rio's expression changed to confusion. "Then why are you so sad, Nurse Sarah? God does only well, sí?"

"Sí, you are right, God does all things well." Sarah smiled. Rio's words and repeating them caused the sword of illumination to hit her heart. She confessed aloud as she rubbed Rio's head, "Out of the mouth of babes."

"I am not a baby," Rio protested.

"No, but you are my dear friend, and God's voice to my ear."

Rio smiled broadly. "I am?"

Sarah smiled through her eyes. "You are."

Rio's face beamed. "I am glad."

Sarah kissed him on the forehead. "Me, too."

Rio's words burned deep into Sarah's heart. Though circumstances had not changed, Rio reminded her that God had not changed, either. She repeated to herself often, "God does only good things," and smiled through her eyes again. She made the active choice to let her faith affect the way she lived and interacted each day.

Providencia   *Deborah A. Hodge*

Over the next months, Ambassador Hodges was faithful to keep in touch but had very little to tell except that the rebels and the seminary were still negotiating a price for Jason's release and the authorities in Colombia were constantly trying to glean information that might lead to Jason's location.

Eight months had passed since Jason's abduction and no new information had come from the rebels. There had been no pictures of Jason released since the first pictures. There had only been negotiations via internet. Roy had kept Sarah informed on the negotiations. The demands had gone from $1 million to $750,000 to $500,000, and finally to $250,000. Roy and the seminary were doing what they could to raise the ransom but were hoping the rebels would negotiate further down.

Sarah thought it strange to put a price tag on a person's value. She prayed constantly about it. "Father, Jason is worth the world to me. How could he be worth a dollar amount to strangers? Please let someone be willing to pay something for his release. Please let someone be willing to pay the rebels' asking price. For Jason's sake, someone has to be willing to pay. Please, Father."

Someone called her name, interrupting Sarah's reflection. She looked up to see Luz coming toward her.

"Luz."

Luz grabbed her and hugged her tightly. "Sarah, I have news."

"News?"

"I have news of Jason."

Wide-eyed, Sarah stepped back. "How?"

Chapter 24

"My brother told me."

Sarah's mouth flew open. "Your brother!"

Luz smiled. "Sí, I went to Colombia and found my brother. I made him tell me about Jason."

Sarah tried to wrap her head around it all. "You went to Colombia."

Luz nodded again. "Sí."

"You found Eduardo."

Luz took Sarah's arm as she nodded. "Sí."

"But, he's the one who kidnapped Jason. Why would he tell you?"

"Because I was right, he didn't understand."

Sarah shook her head trying to understand. "He didn't understand what?"

"He didn't understand about Jason and me, and what kind of man Jason was. I straightened him out."

"How?"

"I told him that Jason was a good man, a godly man, and that I had been a foolish lovesick girl."

"Oh."

"I told him that Jason had tried to help me see the truth, but I had been blind. Eduardo confessed that Jason had tried to tell him that but that he refused to listen. He also told me that he had tried to kill Jason."

A loud gasp interrupted Luz's explanation. Sarah's face was ashen and pale and her mouth open. Luz grabbed her by both arms as she quickly continued, "He was unsuccessful; his leader stopped him. Even so, he and his amigos continued to threaten Jason. They were amazed when Jason told them that even though he did not want to die, he was ready to. They laughed at him, but no matter how they treated him, he didn't fight back. Rather, he prayed for them. They had never seen such a thing."

Sarah repeated with great concern. "No matter how they treated him. How did they treat him?"

Providencia   *Deborah A. Hodge*

Luz looked down and reluctantly admitted, "Not well, I'm afraid. They beat him and starved him."

A look of terror filled Sarah's eyes and face. "What!"

"Sí, they did. They were trying to break his faith, but they did not succeed."

"So, how is he?"

"My brother says he is okay. He's being held in a rebel hideout in the jungle."

Relieved, Sarah probed, "Eduardo told you that."

Luz nodded, "Sí, he did."

"Why did he decide to tell you?"

Luz smiled. "It seems that he and his amigos were so troubled by Jason's words and example that they became ashamed of how they were treating him."

Sarah marveled, "Wow."

"I explained that he and his amigos were under conviction. Eduardo didn't understand so I explained. He confessed that Jason had told him and his other captors repeatedly about his faith, about what God has done for him in his life, and about what Jesus did for everyone so that our sins could be forgiven. Even when Eduardo and the others lashed out at him, Jason continued to act as Jesus teaches, treating them not with hatred but with respect and love. Eduardo and his amigos were amazed. They stopped hating him and began to admire him. I told Eduardo that Jason was acting like Jesus. My brother confessed he had never known a man like Jason and wished that he could be like him. I told him that he could if he accepted Jesus as Savior and Lord. Eduardo nodded and I shared the Gospel with him and he accepted Christ Jesus as his savior."

Sarah eyes lit up with joy. "That's wonderful, Luz."

"It *is* wonderful, but there's more. My brother decided to tell the authorities where to find Jason. They will free Jason shortly."

Sarah grabbed Luz and hugged her tightly. "That's great! That's so great. Thank you, Luz."

Christian walked in as the celebrating was taking place.

Chapter 24

"What's happened?"

"Luz's brother is helping the authorities find Jason. They are on their way to free him."

"That's great!" Christian said with genuine enthusiasm.

Sarah smiled broadly. "It sure is. Is it okay if I leave early so I can tell Mom and Dad?"

Christian nodded. "Sure, go tell them."

Sarah hugged him. "Thanks."

Luz waved bye, as Sarah grabbed her purse and they left.

Rejoicing and praise filled the twenty-minute drive. As Sarah and Luz excitedly burst through the front door with her news, David, Sarah's father, was on the phone.

"Yes, Ambassador Hodges. I'll tell her. Thank you for calling."

As her father hung up, Sarah smiled broadly. "Let me tell you." Her father looked at her mother. "Luz's brother told the authorities where Jason was and they have freed him from the rebels."

Her father's face took on a look of astonishment. He glanced at his wife again.

Luz proudly proclaimed, "My brother accepted Christ. That's why he told the authorities."

Captured by the joy of the moment, Sarah asked, "When will they let us know about Jason's release?"

Her father sighed as he began. "The ambassador called to let us know that the authorities followed up on Eduardo's information, but they arrived too late."

Sarah's joy turned into terror. "Too late, is Jason all right?"

"They weren't there, honey. The rebels had abandoned the camp."

"What?" Luz uttered in disbelief.

"The camp was empty. The rebels had been there but had pulled out a

Providencia   Deborah A. Hodge

short time before the troops arrived."

"But, Eduardo said," Luz's voice trailed off.

"The authorities are hopeful that Eduardo can give them the new location. They made a deal with Eduardo that they would go easy on him if he'd become an informant against FARC and Calberto. Eduardo had gone to the camp before them, and there was no sign of Eduardo either."

"Do they think Eduardo told Calberto that the troops were coming?" Sarah asked.

"They don't know, but they don't think so."

"Eduardo did not warn them; he has truly changed. He has accepted Jesus as his Savior."

Sarah patted Luz, trying to comfort her. Sarah's father and mother tried to comfort both young women.

"They'll get Jason back. It's just a matter of time."

"It's been eight months. I hope it's not eight more."

Everyone nodded.

Chapter 24

Providencia   Deborah A. Hodge

His two guards had rousted Jason out of his bed. As he woke, he realized that frantic activity was taking place outside. Once outside, he observed rebels throwing supplies into trucks. The guards hurried him to a truck and helped him to climb into the back. Once the rebels had packed everything, the trucks sped away.

During the trip, the guards discussed the reason for moving. His Spanish had improved to the point that he understand that a supporter had warned Calberto that the troops were moving against his camp. The supporter told them that the army was only an hour or two behind. Jason's heart sank as he heard that. *Father God, my rescue was so close. Couldn't you have allowed me to be found? Lord couldn't you?*

This silent prayer ended as Eduardo jumped into the back of the truck. "Hello gringo. I see there are no bruises on your face. Did you miss me?" he asked with a laugh. The guards laughed too. Jason only stared at him. Eduardo stared back. What he saw in Eduardo's eyes shocked Jason. He prayed the change he saw to be true.

"I will see you again when we arrive at the new camp." Eduardo said as he leaped from the back of the truck.

Jason pondered the whole event. The tone and the threat were the same as before, but the eyes were different. Exactly what the difference was, Jason didn't know.

At the new camp, the rebels unloaded everything, including Jason, and put it all in its proper place. A guard dragged Jason to his new hut, one less accommodating than the last, which had been his home for more than six months. This time there was no bed, only a mat on the dirt floor. The window was much smaller, and this time the guard chained him to the wall near the mat. Jason settled in and prayed for strength, wisdom and patience to endure. *Lord God, help me please. I feel like the psalmist who* was in the pit, and like him, I cry out to You. Lord I know You listen to me. Help me wait patiently and expectantly until You draw me up out of this horrible pit.

The next morning Eduardo kept his promise. He brought Jason his morning meal of bananas and papaya. He dismissed the guard for breakfast as he came in.

"Hello gringo. I bring you breakfast."

Jason rose up from his mat. "Thank you."

Eduardo glanced to see whether the guard had gone. With the coast clear, he moved closer to Jason. Expecting the beating usually accompanying Eduardo, Jason cringed. Instead of the abuse, Eduardo brought news too good to be true. He leaned over and in a very low tone said, "Señor Jason, I am here to help you escape."

Jason froze, dumbfounded. Eduardo tried again. "Jason, I will help you escape."

Afraid it was a trick, Jason pondered his words for a moment, tilted his head and asked, "Why would you do that?"

Eduardo's face took on an expression unfamiliar to Jason. "I am the one who got you into this, and I will get you out."

Confusion reigned over Jason's face. "I don't understand."

Eduardo explained, "Because of you and Luz, I have become a follower of Jesus Christ."

Surprise and joy flooded Jason's face. "You are a follower of Christ?"

Eduardo nodded and smiled. "I am."

From his face and the tone of his voice, Jason could tell that Eduardo was sincere.

"That's great."

"Yes, it is, and I am so sorry that you are now in the situation that you are because of me."

"I'll be all right."

Eduardo's expression changed. "You don't understand, Señor Jason. Calberto is growing tired of negotiating with your seminary. He may soon see you as expendable."

Providencia *Deborah A. Hodge*

Jason's eyes widened as he rubbed his bearded chin. All he could manage to say was "Wow."

Eduardo touched his arm. "I tried to help you earlier by telling the authorities where you were, but someone warned Calberto that they were coming."

Jason eyes widened. He couldn't believe what he was hearing. "You told the authorities where to find me."

Eduardo peeked to see whether the guard was coming back. "I did, and I will keep trying to free you until I do."

Jason tried to wrap his head around what Eduardo was saying and allow himself to believe that God was finally answering his prayers. "Thank you."

Eduardo saw the guard returning. "We must wait for the right moment."

Jason nodded. As the guard arrived at the front door, Eduardo whispered. "Forgive me, but they must not suspect me." With that, he landed a blow on Jason's jaw. As Jason's head snapped back, the guard stuck his head in the door. Seeing Jason fall back and grab his jaw, the guard laughed and patted Eduardo on the back. Eduardo shot a quick glance in Jason's direction as he left the hut.

Eduardo had landed a hard blow. Even Jason could believe that he had been malicious, except for the words he had whispered before the assault. His aching jaw could not deter his hopefulness. He rehearsed Eduardo's words in his mind. *"I'll help you escape. I got you into this. I'll get you out. I'm a follower of Jesus Christ."* With great joy, Jason quoted Scripture as he uttered a thankful prayer. *This poor man called and the LORD heard him; he saved him out of all his troubles. Thank You, Lord. Please protect Eduardo and give him the wisdom to know when the time is right, and help us to be successful in our escape.*

Days turned into weeks before he saw Eduardo again. The waiting for his return began to diminish his hope. His fears began to take the ascendancy and questions flooded his mind. *What if Eduardo is dead? What if Calberto suspected his intentions and killed him? What if I never get out of this place?*

Circumstances forced him to take himself by the scruff of the neck and refocus his thinking. *Why are you cast down, O my soul? Why are you so disturbed within me? Hope in God for I shall yet praise him, my Savior and God,*

Chapter 25

this poor man cried unto the Lord. He heard me and delivered me from my fears.

He made up his mind to trust God in spite of his fears, and his questions were answered three days later, when once again Eduardo came into the hut bringing breakfast, and again, he dismissed the guard. Jason waited with eager anticipation. Making sure the guard was beyond earshot Eduardo finally spoke. "I am sorry it has taken so long, but I had to make sure they did not suspect me of betraying them."

Jason smiled excitedly. "It's okay; I'm use to waiting."

"But, you will wait no longer. Be ready to go tonight."

Jason could hardly believe it. "Tonight," he repeated.

Eduardo spoke in quiet tones. "Tonight, I will bring your supper and I will release you from your chains. I will give you a knife that you can use to make a hole in the back of the hut. I will watch for you, and I will lead you from the camp and to freedom."

Jason mirrored Eduardo's tones. "How can I ever thank you?"

"There is no need. I am simply righting a wrong."

"But you are risking your life to do it. That takes real courage. Thank you."

Eduardo shook his head. "I may be risking your life as well as mine. There will be no army this time."

"No army," Jason repeated.

Eduardo peeked out the door to see whether the guard was returning. "No army. I am afraid Calberto will find out again. He has informants everywhere."

Jason frowned slightly. "I see. It's okay."

Seeing the guard returning, Eduardo patted Jason's shoulder to encourage him. "Here comes the guard. I will see you tonight."

Jason nodded. "I'll be ready."

"Forgive me again," Eduardo said, as the guard arrived at the door. Once again, he clipped Jason on the jaw. The guard laughed as he enjoyed the entertainment, but he increased his satisfaction by striking Jason himself. Eduardo restrained him from landing another blow. As he

---

Providencia   *Deborah A. Hodge*

grabbed the guard, he laughed and reminded him that the gringo was still worth money. As the two walked out the door, Eduardo glanced back to see Jason picking himself up from the floor and wiping blood from his mouth.

About an hour after they left, Jason began to feel ill. He shivered with cold and burned up with heat as chills and fever began to ravage his body. His head pounded, his body was on fire, and he ached all over. His mind was fuzzy as delirium set in. He lay writhing on his mat as the day passed.

When Eduardo came with his supper, he suspected that Jason had malaria and was sure that he wouldn't be going anywhere that night. He quickly sought help for Jason. He went to the supply hut and retrieved a bottle of quinine and an extra blanket. He grabbed a jug of water and returned to the hut. He gently raised Jason's head and coaxed him to swallow the pills with water.

"Take the medicine. It will make you better."

Jason complied and whispered, "Thank you."

He put a wet cloth on his head and covered him with the blanket that Jason had kicked off, and the new one. Once he had tucked Jason in, he stayed as long as he could without drawing attention. Before he left he whispered, "I'll check on you as often as I can. We'll try our escape plan when you are well enough."

After receiving the medicine, Jason fell asleep and slept for four days. Two weeks would pass before Jason would be well enough to try the escape plan again.

Jason raised his head as Eduardo entered the hut.

"Good, you're awake."

"How long have I been sick?"

"Two weeks!"

"You have been delirious most of the time."

"Delirious?"

"That's the way it is when you have malaria." Eduardo said as he placed the morning meal in front of Jason.

Chapter 25

"I have malaria."

"Yes, but you seem better now."

Jason's hand shook as he lifted his coffee to his mouth. "I feel better, but weak."

Eduardo helped him steady his hand and take a drink. "You haven't eaten very much for two weeks. You'll be stronger after you have eaten today."

Jason swallowed a sip of coffee and asked, "When can we try to escape?"

Eduardo handed him the bread he had brought. "It needs to be soon. Calberto is running out of patience with your seminary."

Jason stopped chewing. "He's ready to get rid of me, huh?"

Eduardo sat back. "I'm afraid so."

"Can we try tonight?"

"I don't think you're well enough."

"I think I am," Jason answered.

Eduardo eyed him as he offered Jason a banana. "You think are, or you know you are?"

Jason grabbed his arm. "I'll be all right. I promise; I'm ready. Please, I have to get out of here."

Eduardo nodded. "Okay, tonight it is. You know the plan. Eat your breakfast and rest. I'll see you tonight." There was no fist upside his face this time. Eduardo left the hut before the guard came back. He waited outside until the guard returned.

Jason ate his food and lay on his mat to rest as Eduardo had suggested. He watched the clouds as they danced by the little window and prayed silently for the success of the escape plan. He quoted Psalm 18:46-48. *"The LORD lives! Praise be to my Rock! Exalted be God my Savior! He is the God who avenges me, who subdues nations under me, who saves me from my enemies. You exalted me above my foes; from a violent man you rescued me."* Father, thank you for Eduardo and his salvation, and for taking care of me thus far. Please give us success in our escape plan and guide us to a place of safety and freedom. Thy will be done, in Jesus' name, amen.

Providencia   *Deborah A. Hodge*

The day passed slowly, but finally the time for the evening meal came. Jason expected Eduardo at any minute, but he did not come. The guard delivered his meal, and the evening shadows began to fall without a trace of Eduardo. Jason's spirit deflated. He wondered whether Eduardo had been suspected and the plan smashed. He sat on his mat, peered through the small window and prayed. *Please, God, let it be tonight.*

In the midst of his prayer, a shadow appeared at the window, tossed something through, and disappeared. The hut was dark except for the sliver of moonlight that shone through the small window. Jason searched the mat and the floor for what had been hurled into the hut. Finally, his fingers discovered a bundle of tied cloth. Gathering it in his hand, he held it toward the moonlight, and carefully opened it to find a key and a knife. Eduardo was keeping his promise. Jason glanced to see where the guard was. He was outside in his usual position and didn't appear to have heard or seen anything. Jason quickly inserted the key into the locks that held him in chains. Once free, Jason quietly moved to the back of the hut and quickly dug for freedom. Quietly and determinedly, he dug for two hours before he created a hole big enough to have a good glimpse outside. Every few minutes he glanced to see whether the guard suspected anything, but the guard never moved. Jason believed it was because the Lord was answering his prayers. Two more hours of digging produced a hole big enough for him to crawl though. He took one more glance toward the guard before poking his head through the hole to look around. He didn't see anyone, so he crawled through.

Outside the hut, he continued on his belly toward the tall grass directly ahead. He inched toward the grass and suddenly saw it move. He froze until Eduardo caught his eye and waved him on. He crawled quickly now and slid into the tall grass, confident that their plan was succeeding. Entering the grass, he was met with shoes and a fresh change of clothes.

Eduardo thrust them into his hands. "Change, quickly."

Jason nodded. "Thanks."

Eduardo watched for any signs of alarm in the camp as Jason changed. Jason was a little weaker than he had thought. As quickly as he could, he shed the rags he wore and put on the clean clothes.

"Hurry," Eduardo admonished.

Jason tried to hurry. He slipped the shoes on. Rubbing his hands across his new clothes, he smiled broadly because he felt like a new man. He hadn't worn shoes and clean clothes for months.

Chapter 25

Jason was ready to go. Eduardo motioned for him to follow him as they crouched low to the ground until they were a couple of miles away. Jason's body was tired and ached. Finally, confident that they had made a clean getaway, they stood up and moved swiftly through the jungle toward the home of a friend that had promised Eduardo that he would help them with transportation to Quito.

Traveling to the home of Eduardo's friend took most of the night. They arrived before dawn only to find the house dark and his truck gone. Eduardo was leery of the circumstances and thought it best not to approach the house. As they reconnoitered at the edge of the clearing, he explained, "This is not good. Ramirez said that he would be here to help us. Something is wrong."

"What do we do?" Jason asked.

"We keep moving. I know the trails. We will take the ones least expected."

"What do we do for food?"

"We will live off the land. It will take longer to get you to a place of real safety, but I promise you that I will. Maybe we can get transportation along the way."

Jason agreed. "Okay, lead the way."

They traveled till the sun rose and then hid and rested through the day. When darkness fell again, they traveled through the moonlit trails chosen by Eduardo. He led the way with confidence. When they heard voices, they hid, knowing the rebels were searching for them and that if they found them, they would immediately execute Eduardo, and most likely Jason also.

Eduardo's knowledge of the trails, water and food sources proved indispensable during the next three weeks as they snuck through the jungle to freedom. They were making good time when the malaria plagued Jason again.

Eduardo noticed that Jason was unable to keep up. "What is wrong?"

Chapter 26

"What?"

"You are not moving as quickly today."

Jason frowned. "Sorry, but I feel a little under the weather."

"You feel what?"

"I'm sorry. I do not feel well today."

Eduardo stopped in his tracks. "Is it the same as before?"

Jason nodded. "I think so. I am cold, then hot, and my head is starting to pound."

Eduardo considered their options and decided. "We need to find a safe place quickly. You are beginning to experience another malaria episode, and we have no quinine."

"Let's try to go on. I can make it a little farther."

"I'm not sure that is a good idea."

"Come on, just a little farther," Jason insisted.

"Okay, but not much. We will stop when I find an appropriate safe place."

Jason nodded, and they trudged on. Eduardo blazed the trail while constantly looking over his shoulder to check on Jason. Jason's pace became slower and slower until it became very apparent that Jason could go no farther. He was dripping with perspiration, coughing and holding his stomach with both hands.

"Why did you stop?" Jason asked.

"You can go no farther, me amigo."

"I can try."

"No Jason."

Suddenly Jason bent over as the vomiting began. Eduardo surveyed the terrain for a suitable hiding place. He spied a thick stand of trees. He helped Jason to the trees, where he constructed a bed of leaves and soft grass by a log. The vomiting slowly subsided, but the chills, fever and pain incapacitated Jason.

Providencia   *Deborah A. Hodge*

Eduardo tried to nurse Jason as best he could. He found fruit and fresh water. He kept him hydrated, tried to force nourishment down him, and covered him with his poncho. However, it was clear in a couple of days that Jason wasn't getting better; he was getting worse.

Knowing that Jason badly needed quinine, Eduardo decided to leave him long enough to try to find some in a nearby village. He built a shelter over Jason with sticks covered with large leaves and grass to provide camouflage. He crawled in and bent over Jason as he lay on the bed of leaves and soft grass. "Jason, can you hear me?"

Jason nodded. Eduardo used his handkerchief to wipe the perspiration from Jason's brow.

"I've built a camouflaged shelter over you in case someone comes by. I'm going to leave you for a while, and try to find some quinine. I'll be back as soon as possible. There's water to your left, along with bananas. Okay?"

Jason nodded again, and answered in a whisper, "Okay."

"Good man. Just rest; I'll be back." He wiped Jason's brow again and left on his quest.

Throughout the morning, Jason drifted in and out of sleep. As he slept, Sarah was with him in his dreams. When he was awake, he quoted Scripture and prayed that Eduardo would be successful in his attempt to find help. As the day crept toward afternoon, his fever inched upward. He became delirious and weak and unable to retrieve and drink the water he needed. As night fell, Eduardo had not returned. The delirium and dehydration brought on unconsciousness. By morning Jason would be barely hanging on to life.

Early the next morning, there was a rustling in the trees accompanied by a bevy of voices. The voices moved closer. Someone spied the shelter, got on his knees to look in and shouted, "Here! He is here." Many hands including Eduardo's quickly tore away the shelter to expose Jason. He knelt down beside Jason.

"Jason, can you hear me?" There was no answer. He checked Jason's pulse. It seemed very weak. Eduardo feared Jason was dying. He swallowed hard and said, "This man is very ill, Capitán. He needs help quickly."

The captain pointed to one of his men. "Médico," he explained.

As the man examined Jason, he quickly agreed with Eduardo's conclusion.

The captain looked at a man with a radio and ordered. "Call for a helicopter."

The man with the radio quickly answered, "Sí, Capitán."

The captain next ordered that stretcher be constructed. The soldiers had provided Eduardo with some quinine. One of the soldiers helped him lift Jason's head, put the quinine in his mouth and pour water in and force Jason to swallow the medicine before they gently lifted him onto the stretcher.

The captain explained, "We must march to a place where the helicopter can land. That is four kilometers to the north."

Eduardo's face revealed his concern. "Okay."

The soldiers moved as quickly as possible. The march took about fifteen minutes. The helicopter was waiting.

The captain yelled to Eduardo as they moved toward the helicopter. "It is a medical helicopter. Your friend will receive assistance as they take him to the hospital in Bogotá."

Eduardo extended his hand. "Gracias Capitán. Dios te bendiga!"

"Vaya con dios," the capitán answered as he shook Eduardo's hand.

The medical personnel quickly assessed Jason's condition, inserted an IV, and monitored his vitals while consulting with the hospital over the radio . The flight took forty-five minutes. When they arrived, hospital personnel rushed to retrieve Jason from the helicopter and hurry him toward the Emergency Department. The doctor made his own assessment, ordered the proper medical protocols, and admitted him to the ICU.

Eduardo also found Ambassador McKinnie and Colombian authorities waiting at the hospital. They were there to make sure Jason received the best medical treatment possible, to congratulate Eduardo, and to debrief him concerning the rebels.

Ambassador McKinnie stuck out his hand. "I am Ambassador McKinnie. It's nice to meet you, Señor Gutierrez. On behalf of the United States of America, I would like to express my country's profound gratitude to you."

Eduardo shook hands. "Thank you, Señor Ambassador."

Señor Estanzo, the Colombian chief official, also offered his hand. "Señor Gutierrez your country also expresses its gratitude."

"Gracias Señor Estanzo. I am very glad Señor Jason is finally free. I hope he will recover from the malaria."

"Sí, I also do. Señor Gutierrez, we need to talk about Calberto's location."

"Sí Señor, but I am sure he has moved the camp."

"That may be so, but we would like to keep a record of the camps. We may catch him later if not now," Señor Estanzo said.

Ambassador McKinnie's phone rang. "Please excuse me," he said as he answered the phone. "Yes, Ambassador Hodges, Dr. Parks is here. He has a severe case of malaria and dehydration. He is in the ICU. The doctor thinks he'll be all right in time ... Right Heather, we were lucky this time ... Right, I'll expect them tomorrow and make arrangements to pick them up. Tell them I'll have someone meet them at the airport and drive them to the hospital."

Sarah, her parents and Luz arrived the following day. They found Eduardo in the ICU waiting room.

Luz hurried to greet her brother. "Eduardo, I am so proud of you."

Eduardo hugged her. "Thank you, Luz."

Sarah smiled. "No, we all thank *you*."

Sarah's parents added, "We owe you so much."

"I owe Jason so much," he said as he put his arm around his sister, "And Luz. It is because of them that I know Jesus."

Luz smiled broadly. Sarah, her parents and Eduardo joined in. They all broke into joyous laughter.

"How is Jason?" Sarah asked.

"He was not good when he came here. He was barely alive. I was

Chapter 26

afraid he would die."

Sarah's eyes popped with alarm. "How is he now? "

"The doctor says he is better; they have taken very good care of him."

"That's good," Sarah said, fighting tears of relief. Sarah closed her eyes and silently thanked God. Cate, her mother, realizing what she was doing, put her arm around her daughter and drew her close, and whispered, "He's all right." Sarah nodded as her tears won the battle. "He will be fine, Sarah. God has answered our prayers."

Sarah nodded again, as tears of relief seeped from the corners of her still closed eyes.

"Yes, He has."

Providencia   *Deborah A. Hodge*

Once Jason's doctor became aware of the arrival of the Barnes family, he made his way to the area where they were waiting.

"Hello, everyone. I am Dr. Villares. I have been treating Dr. Parks."

Thrusting his hand forward, Sarah's father introduced everyone. "Nice to meet you Dr. Villares. I am David Barnes; this is my wife, Cate, my daughter, Sarah, and our friend Luz Gutierrez. How is Jason today?"

"He is improving."

"That's good."

"Yes, he was at the point of death when he came to us." Realizing the distressed looks on everyone's face, Dr. Villares quickly added, "He has been steadily improving. You see because of the fever from the malaria and the lack of water for almost twenty-four hours, he was very dehydrated when he arrived. We have been replenishing his electrolytes intravenously."

Sarah spoke up. "Dr. Villares, I am a nurse. I understand what you are saying."

"Then you know that the protocol will take time to have the desired effect."

Sarah nodded. "I do."

"The starvation that he experienced during his captivity has complicated the situation."

Sarah choked her feelings and tried to sound very professional. "So the protocol will take longer to produce the desired results."

"Yes, but maybe not so long."

"How long do you expect him to be in the ICU?"

"I am hoping for only two to three more days. We shall take it day by day. Visiting time is in another hour, but you all can see him now if you wish."

Sarah looked at the others. Everyone nodded. Dr. Villares led the way.

"Is he lucid at all?" Sarah asked.

"I am afraid not. His fever is still high and he is somewhat delirious." Dr. Villares stopped and turned toward everyone. "I know it's been almost a year since you have seen Dr. Parks. I want to prepare you. I am sure he looks quite different from when you saw him last."

Sarah sighed; everyone nodded and proceeded to Jason's room. Dr. Villares' warning was an understatement. As they entered, everyone was shocked to see the emaciated, long-haired, long-bearded figure in the bed. Sarah felt her legs give way. Her parents, who flanked her, kept her from falling. They ushered her to a nearby chair.

Dr. Villares apologized. "I'm sorry. I tried to warn you."

"It's fine, Dr. Villares," David answered.

"I thought I knew what to expect, but …." A groan interrupted Sarah's statement. Everyone turned their focus to the patient in the bed. Jason let out another groan. Dr. Villares moved quickly toward the bed. Jason's face was pinched and he was perspiring profusely. The doctor found a damp wipe and swabbed his brow. Realizing that Jason was moving his lips, the doctor bent down to try to hear. Unable to discern what Jason was saying, Dr. Villares inquired, "Dr. Parks can you open your eyes?" There was no response. "Dr. Parks can you hear me?" The doctor took his light and checked the reactivity of Jason's pupils. Then he looked at the others and shook his head.

"He isn't lucid."

"But he sounds as if he's hurting," Sarah said.

Jason let out another groan, a louder one. Dr. Villares checked his IV. "Everything seems to be fine." He checked his chart. "He receives medicine for pain every six hours and it's only been three."

"Should we go so you can check him over, Doctor?" David asked.

Providencia   Deborah A. Hodge

"That might be a good idea, Mr. Barnes. If you will sit outside for a moment, you can come back in when I am finished."

The four of them quietly left the room.

Sarah voiced her fears. "I'm afraid something else is going on with Jason besides the malaria."

"Let's just wait and see what Dr. Villares says," her dad suggested.

Sarah dropped her head. Her nurse's brain was working and it was telling her that nothing was good.

Five minutes later, Dr. Villares cracked the door and asked them to come back in.

"I didn't find anything, but to be safe, I'll order an ultrasound."

Sarah inquired, "So you suspect ...." Once again, a groan interrupted.

"I'm beginning to suspect something," Dr. Villares quickly added.

"What?" Sarah asked. Once again, there was a groan.

Dr. Villares motioned for Sarah to follow him. Sarah followed obediently.

The other occupants of the room watched. "Miss Barnes, you said that you are a nurse, correct?"

"That's correct." There was a groan accompanied by a frown on the patient's face.

Watching Jason's face, Dr. Villares asked another question. "How long have you been a nurse?"

"Four years."

A loud groan and grimace punctuated her answer. The groan was so loud that Sarah jumped. "Would you be kind enough to check the patient's pulse?"

Sarah's eyes revealed her confusion. The doctor nodded his seriousness. "Of course, Doctor." Another loud, sustained groan and grimace bracketed her reply. However, the moment Sarah touched Jason's wrist to check his pulse, the groaning ceased and the grimace subsided. His pulse was extremely rapid when she first took his wrist, but steadily slowed as she continued.

Chapter 27

Everyone noticed the difference. Dr. Villares stroked his chin and nodded. "Exactly as I suspected, Miss Barnes. It's you."

"Me?" Sarah replied, still holding Jason's wrist.

Dr. Villares nodded again. "Yes, first it was your voice and then your touch."

"Really."

"How was his pulse when you first took his wrist?"

"Rapid."

"How is it now?"

"Normal."

"And, you're still holding his wrist."

"Oh." Sarah self-consciously replied as she dropped his hand.

Dr. Villares pointed to Jason's face. "See."

Sarah could easily see that the grimace had reappeared. She gently took his hand and the pain in his face melted away.

"Wow! Sarah, he knows you are here," Luz said.

Sarah sighed. "But he's not lucid."

"Maybe not, honey, but some part of his unconscious mind knows you are here," Cate assured her.

Sarah glanced at Dr. Villares. "Your mother is right. Though he is not lucid, somehow he knows you are here."

Sarah could not contain her emotions. She tried hard to choke them into submission, but she could not corral the torrent of tears that streamed from her eyes. Her mother quickly consoled her. "It's okay Sarah. It's been a rough year."

Sarah buried her face in her mother's shoulder and let the floodgates open. Her father helped gently lead her from the room. Luz and Dr. Villares followed.

"I'm sorry, Miss Barnes. I did not mean to upset you. His knowledge of your presence is a good thing. I believe it will make him fight harder to get better."

Sarah couldn't choke back the tears enough to answer. "Thank you, Dr. Villares. My daughter's tears are tears of relief and joy, not sadness."

"Oh, I see. You all are welcome to go back in and stay a little longer or come back in an hour for regular visiting hours. I think it will do Dr. Parks good to have you there."

"Thank you, Doctor."

"You are welcome. I will see you later." With that, Dr. Villares moved to the nurses' station, gave a few words of instruction and was gone.

"Sarah, would you like to go back in or wait until visiting hours?" Cate asked, as she tenderly held her daughter.

"I'd like to go back in."

"Would you like to have company or go in alone?"

"I'd like to be alone if that's okay."

"Sure," her mom answered.

Both her dad and Luz gave her a consoling pat as they headed for the waiting room. Sarah forced a smile as her mother reassured her, "Everything's going to be okay."

Sarah sniffed and wiped her eyes and face. "I know."

"See you in a few minutes or at visiting time," Cate said, as she squeezed her daughter's hand and turned to walk to the waiting room.

Sarah moved toward the door of Jason's room, stopped, took a deep breath, let it out slowly, turned the knob and walked in. She stopped at the foot of the bed, retrieved his chart and, thinking like a nurse, she reviewed information. Moving closer to the patient, she continued her observation of every detail of the patient's appearance and medical care. She checked the IV, the bags of medicine, the monitoring of his vitals by the machine. She felt his brow. Satisfied with the information she had gleaned, she sat down beside his bed, folded her hands and began to pray silently. *Father, I thank you so much that Jason is free and is doing much better physically. I know there is no cure for malaria, but please help him get over this episode and learn to cope with the disease. Father, I believe you have been helping me understand that in Your providence You have brought Jason and me together again because it is Your will that we be married. I don't know*

Chapter 27

if You have brought Jason to that same conclusion or not, but I ask You please to bring us both to the same conclusion if it is really Your will for us to be together. In Jesus' name, I pray. Amen.

As she finished her prayer, she placed her right hand on Jason's arm, laid her head back, closed her eyes, and went to sleep. A nurse woke her as she came in to check on Jason.

"You are Miss Barnes, the nurse?" she inquired.

Sarah sat upright and brushed her hair from her face. "I am."

"He is much better."

"That's good."

As she wrote on his chart, the nurse added, "His vitals have much improved since you arrived. You must be very important to him."

Sarah smiled, "Well, he's very important to me."

The nurse smiled. "Sí, that is evident. Please let us know if you need anything."

"Gracias," Sarah said, as she looked at the nurse's nametag, "Cari."

"De nada, Miss Barnes."

"Sarah, my name is Sarah."

"De nada, Sarah."

As the nurse exited, Sarah settled back down in her chair, repositioned her right hand on Jason's arm, and drifted back to sleep.

Luz, Eduardo and her parents woke her again as they came in for visiting time.

"How is he?" they inquired.

"The nurse tells me that his vitals are much better."

"That's great, honey," her parents responded.

"He has much better medicine now," Eduardo added.

Luz continued, "Eduardo means you, Sarah."

Providencia   Deborah A. Hodge

Sarah blushed. "I'm just glad he's getting better."

Chapter 27

Providencia   *Deborah A. Hodge*

The next day, Dr. Villares ordered that Jason be moved to a private room. He still had a fever and delirium, but he was no longer dehydrated. Sarah consulted the doctor, "How is he really doing, Doctor?"

Dr. Villares explained, "In Dr. Park's type of malaria dehydration is a serious concern, but that has been reversed. I am confident that by continuing to follow the proper medical protocol he will soon recover. We can expect his fever to rise and fall for a week or two. During these episodes, he will continue to experience aches and pains with the fever, followed by deep sleep for a period of hours or even days."

Pointing to her parents and Luz and Eduardo, she asked, "Is there anything we can do to make him more comfortable?"

"Your being here has seemed to make him much more comfortable."

Sarah blushed.

Dr. Villares continued, "He is noticeably much less agitated. That helps him and us."

Sarah nodded.

"As a nurse, of course, you can watch his vitals, call the nurses when he needs them, wipe his brow, and see that he drinks water. As for the rest of you, you can be here for him. After his ordeal, I'm sure seeing familiar faces will help him tremendously."

Everyone nodded.

"It is good that he has such good friends," Dr. Villares said, "Call me if you need me?"

"Thank you, Dr. Villares."

David thrust his hand forward. "We appreciate all that you have done."

"You are welcome, but I am only doing my job."

David nodded toward Sarah. "I think you are doing more, Dr. Villares. Thanks for letting Sarah stay with Jason."

Dr. Villares smiled. "Sometimes the practice of medicine involves more than medicines."

"You are a wise doctor," Cate added.

"Thank you, Mrs. Barnes. I will leave you now, but I will see you when I make my rounds tomorrow."

"Well, how about we all take turns sitting with Jason?" David suggested.

"I'll stay tonight Dad. You all go get some rest," Sarah said.

"Honey, you stayed last night. Shouldn't you get some rest tonight?" Cate protested.

"I'll be glad to stay," David offered.

"I'm okay," Sarah protested.

Her parents shot a concerned glance at each other. Before they could say a word, Sarah spoke. "I'll be fine. Please, I want to stay."

"Okay, but one of us will relieve you first thing in the morning," her dad said.

"I will be here very early in the morning so you can go to the hotel and rest," Eduardo responded.

Sarah nodded. Her parents gave her a peck on the cheek. Luz hugged her, and Eduardo waved goodbye.

Once again, it was just Jason and her. She was right where she was supposed to be. She settled down in a chair by his bed, positioned her hand on his arm and sat back to keep an eye on him.

Sarah watched carefully as Jason's fever rose from 103 to 105. She called the nurse, who gave him medicine through his IV while Sarah put a wet, cool cloth on his forehead. She continued to watch his fever and his vitals and got very little sleep.

Providencia   *Deborah A. Hodge*

When Eduardo arrived at 6 am to relieve her, she refused to go.

"This is a bad episode. I am a nurse. I need to be here."

"But, Sarah."

Sarah pleaded. "I need to be here."

"Sarah, I can see that you are tired. I am not sure that your parents would agree."

"I'll handle my parents. My parents will understand."

"Okay, Sarah. I will tell them. We'll be back later."

Sarah touched Eduardo's arm. "Thank you."

"You are welcome, Sarah."

Jason's high fever continued throughout the day.

Eduardo, Luz and her parents arrived later that morning. They brought her something to eat, and insisted that she eat it. Eduardo took over and wiped Jason's brow with a cold cloth while she ate. Once she had finished eating, she returned to her duties.

Throughout the day, the others took turns relieving her. When it became apparent that Jason's episode would continue through the night, and realizing how tired Sarah was, her parents insisted that she not stay that night. Sarah protested, "I'm fine."

However, they were resolute. "Sarah you're going to make yourself sick. You can't stay tonight."

Sarah prepared to protest more adamantly. Eduardo volunteered, "Sarah I will stay. I know what to watch for and how to care for him. You sleep tonight. I will be here and I will call you if anything changes."

Sarah did not want to agree, but didn't know how to graciously turn down Eduardo's offer a second time. "Okay, but I'll see you early in the morning."

Eduardo smiled and nodded. "Sí, hasta mañana."

After everyone left, Eduardo checked Jason's temperature: 104. He removed the cloth from Jason's forehead, wet it and replaced it. *Jason, me*

Chapter 28

amigo, it is clear that Sarah loves you very much. You are a very lucky man."

Like Sarah, Eduardo spent the night watching Jason, calling the nurse, and sleeping very little. This pattern continued for five more days and nights, Eduardo and Sarah taking turns, Eduardo staying every other night.

On the sixth day, though his eyes wouldn't quite focus, Jason regained clarity, and he became aware that he was in a hospital bed. As he tried to get his eyes to focus, he could make out Eduardo sitting in the chair by his bed. "Eduardo, where am I?"

Eduardo stood up. "You are in a hospital in Bogotá. God answered my prayers and I came upon an army patrol when I was looking for the quinine. I guided them to where you were. You were near death when we found you."

Jason let out a big "Wow."

"Sí, there was a paramedic with the patrol. The capitán in charge had him check your condition. When he found that your condition was very bad, the capitán called for a helicopter and had us transported to Bogotá and the hospital. You've been here for almost two weeks."

Jason rubbed his eyes. "Two weeks?"

"Sí, and you have visitors."

"Visitors," he repeated as he raised his head to look around.

"Hello, Jason," Luz said, as she came into his line of vision.

Jason smiled. "Hi, Jason," Sarah added, as she moved to where he could see her.

"Sarah," Jason spoke softly.

Sarah moved close to his bed and took his hand. "How are you?"

He squeezed her hand. "Much better now."

"You were quite sick when they brought you here," Luz added, as she moved toward the bed.

Jason rubbed his face. "I remember being very ill and wondering if

Eduardo would ever come back."

"I'm sorry, me hermano. I came back as quickly as I could."

Sarah responded. "You were very bad when you arrived at the hospital. You were dehydrated and unconscious. Your fever was extremely high and the malaria was not responsive to quinine or anything else for a while. You were in the ICU for four days, but you're better now."

Jason blew out a breath, "Yes, I'm better now."

A knock on the door interrupted their conversation. It was David and Cate, Sarah's parents, and Ambassador McKinnie.

"I'm Ambassador McKinnie, Dr. Parks. I'm glad to see that you're better."

"Thank you. It's nice to meet you, sir," Jason answered.

"Someone from my office and the Colombian authorities will need to debrief you when you feel up to it."

"Debrief me?"

"Yes, we need to know exactly how you were treated and what you can tell us about Calberto and the rebels."

Jason glanced at Eduardo. Eduardo nodded his approval. "Yes sir."

"That's great, and I'll make arrangements for you to go home as soon as you're strong enough."

Jason cut his eyes toward Sarah. There was a frown on her face. He turned his attention back to the ambassador. "Thank you, sir."

"Roy White is coming to escort you back home," David added.

Jason smiled. "It'll be good to see Roy."

"He'll be glad to see you too. Everyone at the seminary was ecstatic when they heard the news of your escape," Cate said.

"It's good to see you, Mr. and Mrs. Barnes."

"It's a blessing to see you," Cate said.

"And an answer to prayer," David added.

Chapter 28

"Many prayers," Jason responded.

"I'm sorry, but I must be going," Ambassador McKinnie said, stretching his hand toward Jason.

Jason shook his hand. "Thanks for coming by, Ambassador McKinnie."

"Let me know if there's anything I can do for you."

He glanced at Sarah again. She was still holding his hand, and this time their eyes met. "Yes sir, thank you."

"Goodbye for now."

"Goodbye, sir."

The ambassador said goodbye to everyone else, and left.

Cate and David had noticed the hand-holding and decided to give them some privacy.

"We were about to go get a bite to eat. Luz, Eduardo, would you like to go with us?"

Eduardo nodded and Luz thankfully agreed. "Yes, thank you, that would be nice."

"Sarah?"

"Thanks Mom, but I think I'll keep an eye on Jason."

"We'll bring you something back."

"That'll be great. Thank you."

The ladies gathered their purses, and everyone took their leave. For the first time in ten months, Jason and Sarah were in the same room and alone. She was sitting beside his bed holding his hand and it seemed like a dream to both of them. Jason held tightly to her hand. He was afraid she would disappear. Realizing what he was doing, Sarah smiled.

"You're safe now." She felt his forehead. "You still have some fever, but you're getting better. There was a time not long ago when we all thought we might never see you again."

"Yeah, me too."

"Was it bad?"

"At times."

Sarah nodded, "Eduardo told us. I'm sorry."

"It's okay; the Lord was with me."

"It's obvious they didn't feed you well. You're skin and bones."

"I ate enough to survive."

Sarah touched his forehead again. "When did you get the malaria?"

He closed his eyes and savored the moment. Her hand felt soothing and wonderful on his forehead. "About three months ago, I think."

"There's no cure for it, you know."

"I know."

"It'll be a constant reminder of what you've been through."

"I know, and that's not necessarily a bad thing."

"Huh?"

"It will be a reminder of God's providence and His faithful sustaining grace."

She brushed his hair with her fingers. "Yeah, He has been faithful hasn't He, and constantly working behind the scenes?"

"I need a haircut." He rubbed his beard. "And a shave."

Sarah smiled. "If you feel up to it, I could help you out with one of those if I had scissors and a razor."

Jason pushed the call button. A nurse answered in Spanish. Sarah requested scissors, a razor and shaving cream. "¿Tiene las cosas para quitar una barba muy larga?" Very shortly, the nurse complied. Sarah slipped her ring off her finger, put it in her pocket. She filled a plastic basin with water, retrieved a towel from the bathroom and raised the head of the bed, and as she draped the towel around his neck she confessed, "I've never really shaved a long beard before."

Jason smiled. "Neither have I. This is the first time I've had a beard in all my life."

Chapter 28

Sarah made a face. "I don't know how to begin to shave a beard this long."

Jason mirrored her face. "This will be a first for both of us. I've never had anyone shave me." They laughed. He felt his beard again. "I think you trim as much as you can and then shave the rest."

"Okay, maybe I should spread the extra sheet over you so I won't get hair everywhere."

Once she spread the sheet, Sarah began with a snip here and a snip there until the face looking back at her resembled the one she knew. She finished the job by spreading a thick layer of shaving cream over his face. Guided by Jason, she very carefully made slow strokes with the razor.

With the last stroke of the razor, she grabbed a washcloth and wiped away the remainder of the shaving cream. After which she took a step back and reviewed her work. She took his face in her hand and made mysterious faces as she analyzed the result of her first shave. Finally, she smiled.

"Pret-ty good job if I do say so myself."

"Is that right?"

"Yep. It's a little thinner, but that's the face I remember."

Jason joked, "Now, if you could just do something about my hair."

Sarah's eyes narrowed and she bit her lip. "I could try."

Wide-eyed, Jason said, "You're serious."

Sarah nodded. "I could take a little of the length off if you trust me to do it."

Jason laughed. "My hair is in your hands."

Sarah carefully removed the sheet and towel, shook them out in the wastebasket, raised the head of the bed more, and draped Jason again before she began snipping.

Jason squirmed. "Don't get carried away."

Sarah grabbed his head. "Keep your head still, please."

Jason froze. "Okay, but are you sure you know what you're doing?"

Providencia   Deborah A. Hodge

Sarah laughed. "Sure, I've done this millions of times."

Jason tried to look around. "Nice to know."

Sarah grabbed his head and turned it back around. "Be still."

"Yes ma'am."

Sarah moved from the back to side-to-side and front as she snipped and combed for twenty minutes. She finally stopped and retrieved a mirror from her purse. She handed it to Jason. He took a look. He rubbed his head and face and smiled. "You're a multi-talented young woman — a nurse and a barber, too."

Sarah smiled. "Thank you, kind sir."

"No, thank you," Jason said. "I feel more like myself than I have in months. If I could just take a shower, I'd be all the way myself."

"Is that right?"

"Yeah, it is."

"I'm not sure that you're strong enough for that."

"Maybe not, but I'd sure like to try."

"Okay, we'll give it a shot."

Sarah pushed the call button and asked the nurse for a handicap chair and a male assistant. The assistant helped Jason with the shower while the nurse changed his bed and Sarah checked to see if he could take on some broth.

Chapter 28

Providencia   *Deborah A. Hodge*

The shower did wonders. Though he had used part of his water rations to wash himself at least once a week, this was the first time he'd felt warm water flow over his body in almost a year. It felt deliciously wonderful. The male assistant had provided him with a chair so he showered for twenty minutes, after which he put on clean underwear and hospital gown, thanked the male orderly, and reported to bed.

"I never realized anything could feel so good."

Sarah fluffed his pillows. "You do look better."

"I feel a lot better."

Sarah checked his forehead. "You may have overdone it. You feel like you have a fever." She poked the thermometer in his mouth. "101, to be exact."

Jason sniffed as he spied the tray. "What is that I smell?"

"Chicken broth, would you like some?"

"Yes, please."

"Why don't you lie back and let me feed it to you?"

"Wow, the royal treatment!"

Sarah took his shoulders and pushed him back. "No, the sick treatment."

"But I'm better."

She prepared to feed him the broth. "Better, but not well. Open wide."

Jason obediently opened his mouth. Sarah spooned broth into it. He

Chapter 29

closed his mouth and swallowed. "Umm."

"Good, huh?"

She spooned another mouthful. "Uh-huh." He gulped each spoonful down so quickly that she couldn't deliver them fast enough, and the meal was over much too soon for Jason.

Pouting like a small boy, he protested, "That's all?"

"That's enough for now. We don't want to overdo it."

"I don't think we could overdo it."

Sarah patted his shoulder. "Trust me. We can. We need to let your body adjust."

"Okay, Nurse Sarah. I'll bow to your advice."

"It's your doctor's advice, not mine."

"Who is my doctor?"

"Dr. Villares. He seems very good."

Jason stealthily changed the subject. He asked the question he had wanted to ask. "How long have you been here, Sarah?"

"For eleven days. Luz, my parents and I came the second day you were here."

"Where's Christian?"

Sarah's eyes narrowed. "He's in Otavalo."

"What does he think about you being here?"

"He's fine with it."

Jason was puzzled. He repeated, "He's fine with it."

She repeated, "He's fine with it. He knows you and I are friends."

Friends ... I wish I could tell you how much I love you. Jason took a deep breath before he replied. "Yes, we are friends. We've known each other for a long time."

"Yes, we have. Christian knows that, and he prayed for you the whole

Providencia   *Deborah A. Hodge*

time you were held captive. He rejoiced with the rest of us when you were rescued."

"He's a great guy, Sarah. You're lucky."

"He is a great guy, and so are you."

Jason smiled and looked her in the eyes. *I love you so much, and if it weren't for Christian, I'd tell you.* He voiced the only reply he could. "Thank you, and thank you for being here."

Sarah took his hand. "I wouldn't have it any other way." Jason searched her eyes to see exactly what she meant. He thought he saw something from the old days. *Oh, God, I'm going to tell her how I feel.* He was poised to make his confession when someone rapped on the door. Dr. Villares entered with Jason's chart.

"They told me you were alert. I am Dr. Villares."

"Nice to meet you, Doctor."

"And you, how are you today, Miss Barnes?" he asked while poking the thermometer in Jason's mouth. "I'm fine, Doctor," Sarah answered.

The doctor checked the thermometer, "Still a fever, but improving. Did you eat your broth?"

"Every drop," Jason answered.

"And wanted more," Sarah added.

"That is very good. I understand that you took a shower, and I see that you have had a shave and a haircut."

"It was all wonderful."

"I'm sure. If you have no more episodes, I suspect we will only keep you a couple of more days, but you must take it easy after that."

"That's great, Doctor."

"I imagine that you are anxious to get back to the United States."

"I am, Doctor." Sarah cringed at that answer. Jason noticed through a side glance.

The doctor started toward the door but turned to add, "I will check on you again tomorrow. I may allow you soft food tomorrow. Let the nurses

Chapter 29

know if you need anything."

"Thank you, Doctor."

As the door closed, Jason tried to screw up his courage to ask Sarah pointedly about her feelings for him. Sarah derailed his intentions.

"Wow, it sounds like you'll be back in the states by the end of the week."

"Yeah, maybe."

"I'm sure you're ready to get back and get on with your life."

God, what should I say? "I'm sure you're ready to get back to Otavalo and get on with yours."

Sarah smiled but didn't answer.

He didn't know how to interpret her silence so he changed the subject. "How's Rio?"

Sarah smiled. "He's great. He knows how to keep me straight."

"What do you mean?"

"He caught me struggling with God's providence and nailed me on it. He asked me, 'Doesn't God do all things well?'"

"How old is he?"

"Five."

Jason chuckled. "Five."

Sarah laughed also. "He's five going on fifteen."

"He's a smart little guy, huh?"

"Very smart."

"So, you have two great guys in your life?"

"Yeah."

The conversation and Sarah's silence baffled Jason. He didn't know how to continue. He couldn't tell if she loved him or Christian. He'd noticed she wasn't wearing a ring, but if she was no longer engaged why wouldn't she mention it? He decided to give it a rest and pray about it.

"I'm a little tired. I think I'm going to take a nap."

"Okay," Sarah answered as she felt his forehead. "You don't seem to have much fever."

"I'm okay; I just need a nap." He pulled the covers over him and turned away so he could pray in private. He fell asleep praying.

While he was sleeping, Sarah read a book but spent most of her time watching him sleep. She wondered whether it was the time to tell him the truth about Christian. Should she tell him how she felt about him? She was afraid to tell him. He had given her no indication that what Rachael had told her was true. She was very confused. Over the last few months, she had begun to believe that God did want them together. She had expected God to lead Jason to that conclusion too, but there was no indication that He had. She didn't know what to think or do.

A knock on the door prevented any further probing of feelings, and also roused Jason. Cate, David, Luz, and Eduardo were back with Sarah's food.

"Wow, you guys have been busy while we were gone," Cate said.

"Yes, you look like the old Jason," Luz added.

Jason grabbed his chest. "Old."

"You know what I mean," Luz answered.

Jason laughed. "I do. Thank you."

"You seem much better," David observed.

"A shave, haircut, shower, clean clothes and broth worked wonders."

"Evidently," Eduardo said with a smile.

Cate handed Sarah her food. She peeked in the bag. "My favorite, thanks."

"What is it?" Jason asked.

Recognizing the tone, Sarah answered, "Something you can't have."

Chapter 29

"But it smells so good." Jason sounded like a little boy.

Cate smiled. "You are much better, aren't you?"

Jason nodded, "Yes, ma'am."

"Who did you find to give you a haircut and a shave?" David asked.

"Sarah."

"Sarah!" Cate exclaimed with a chuckle. "I didn't know you could do all of that, honey."

Sarah grinned. "Neither did I."

"I liked you better with the beard and long hair," Eduardo said.

"Really," Luz responded.

Eduardo laughed. "No, not really."

"I guess we are going to head back to the hotel. Are you coming, Sarah?" David asked.

Sarah stopped chewing and looked at Jason and then back at her parents. "I think I'll stay here at least for a while. He's still running a fever. It might spike again."

"Okay, I guess we'll see you later," her dad said. "Luz, Eduardo, are you ready?"

"Sí, Jason we will see you tomorrow," they both answered.

Cate walked over to Sarah to kiss her goodbye. As she bent down, Sarah whispered, "I'll see you tomorrow, Mom."

"Okay," her mother whispered back. She walked over and kissed Jason on the forehead. "Glad you are feeling better. I'll see you tomorrow."

"Thanks, Mrs. Barnes."

Cate patted his arm and joined the others as they walked through the door.

Jason begged, "Are you sure I can't have some of what you're eating? It smells so good."

"It wouldn't be good for you," Sarah answered as she took a bite.

He poked out his lip and pouted. "Just a little bite?"

Sarah shook her head. "It's too spicy for a stomach that hasn't had solid food for almost two weeks."

Jason continued to pout. "I haven't had spicy food in a year. Please, just a little bite."

Sarah grinned at his poor little boy routine. "Poor baby."

He begged. "Please, just a taste if not a bite."

Sarah yielded, "Okay just a taste."

Sarah took the broth spoon and put a taste on the tip. "Here you go."

Jason opened his mouth wide and savored the taste. "Wow! That's good. Are you sure I can't have another taste?"

Sarah frowned playfully. "Don't push it, buddy. I shouldn't have given you that one. I'll get you your very own meal when the doctor says that you can have solid food."

"Is that a promise?"

Sarah smiled. "It's a promise."

"I'm glad you stayed."

Sarah joked. "Yeah, you wanted my food."

Chapter 30

Jason reached out his hand. "No, I wanted your company. I feel better when you're here."

Sarah stopped chewing, and swallowed. *Is this it Lord?* Sarah wiped her mouth and took his hand. "Why?"

"Why what?"

Here we go again. She put him on the spot. "Why do you feel better when I'm here?"

"I guess it's your bedside manner."

"Any old nurse would do for that."

Jason joked. "I don't want any old nurse. I want you."

She was not amused. *Why do you want me?* She asked him pointedly, "Very funny. Why do you want me here?"

He frowned. "Sarah I was around strangers who did not treat me well for a year. I need to see a familiar face. I need to be with a friend. Is that okay?"

Though not what she wanted to hear, his confession touched Sarah; tears filled her eyes, and she decided to be satisfied with his answer. "Yeah, it's okay."

He closed his eyes. "My head is pounding. I think I need to sleep."

"Would you like for me to get something for your head?"

Jason nodded.

Sarah pushed the call button and requested something for a headache. The nurse quickly obliged. She poked the thermometer in his mouth. "103, his fever is going up again."

Sarah nodded. "I thought so."

The nurse offered something for his headache and the fever. Jason took the pills, thanked the nurse, and closed his eyes again. Sarah thanked the nurse, moved her chair closer to the bed, and checked Jason's forehead. He had begun to shiver so she tucked the covers tightly around him and stroked his head until the shivering calmed down. When she started to remove her hand, Jason grabbed her hand and held on. Without opening his eyes, he clasped her hand and drew it to his

Providencia   *Deborah A. Hodge*

side. Neither one uttered a word. Sarah prayed silently as she scooted her chair closer, sat down and watched as he fell asleep. *God help me. I don't understand. I thought that You wanted us to be together, but Jason doesn't seem to think that. If he loves me, he won't say it. Nothing seems to have changed with him.*

Once he was asleep, she tried to retrieve her hand, but her efforts roused him from his sleep and he held on. She sighed and had to be satisfied with reading a book one-handed. She eventually fell asleep with her head on the side of his bed. However, Jason awakened her as he talked in his sleep and thrashed around in his bed. He cried out as if someone was pursuing him. She rubbed his head and face, as she spoke to him in hushed tones to assure him that everything was all right. He never woke up, but he did calm down. She tried to retrieve her hand again, but he held on for dear life. So she lay her head back down on his bed again and drifted back to sleep.

Chapter 30

Providencia   *Deborah A. Hodge*

The rest of the night was uneventful, and Jason slept most of the next day. He awoke to find Sarah sleeping on the side of his bed. He was still holding her hand. He relished the feeling of her hand in his. He reached with his other hand and touched her hair, and thanked God that she was there. *God I want to thank you that I am free, and that Sarah is here. Father, I love her so much. Please show me what to do. Please show us your will for her life and mine. I cannot believe we have been through all this just to be separated again. Please, Father, don't let her marry another man. Please let her marry me. Please, God, make it possible if it is Your will. Oh, God, Thy will be done.*

Tears filled his eyes as he prayed, and he moved his hands to catch the tears dripping from his eyes. The withdrawal of his hand woke Sarah. As she raised her head, she saw Jason's tears. "What's wrong?"

Jason turned away. Sarah stood up. "What's wrong, Jason? Are you all right? Are you in pain?"

Jason shook his head. "No, I'm okay."

She squeezed his hand. "You're not okay. Can I help?"

He shook his head. "Only God can help." Tears trickled freely from his eyes.

Sarah was distressed. She walked to the other side of the bed so she could see his face. "Why are you crying? Tell me about it. Maybe I can help."

Jason swallowed hard, clenching his teeth and jaw in an effort to choke the flow of tears. He closed his eyes so Sarah couldn't see his pain. His efforts were made more difficult as she stroked his face.

"Please, Jason, let me help you," Sarah pleaded.

Chapter 31

Jason swallowed tears and stated forcefully, "I'm all right."

"I don't believe you, and it might help if you talked about it."

Jason shook his head. "I don't think so."

Sarah held his face in her hands, and tenderly said, "Open your eyes; look at me."

Jason swallowed hard, sighed and opened his eyes. He looked at her momentarily but turned away to try to hide the truth.

Sarah squeezed his face and demanded, "Jason, look at me! Tell me what's wrong."

He reluctantly looked at her. She bent down and forced him to look her in the eyes. He could not hold back the tears. Sarah held his face in one hand and wiped tears with the other. Tears found their way into her eyes, too. Jason reached up to wipe tears that trickled from her eyes. She leaned over and he took her in his arms. They cried together for a few minutes. Finally the crying was over, but he continued to hold Sarah tightly because she seemed to be content in his arms. He stroked her hair as she lay across his chest. She raised her head and looked into his eyes. He gave in to his desire to pull her close and kiss her. She kissed back. He found himself lost in the kiss. She came up for air, and he kissed her again. Five years of loving her and missing her were poured into those kisses and she was responding. Suddenly, he came to his senses and broke it off.

"I'm sorry. I shouldn't have done that."

Sarah looked at him. "You didn't do that. We did that. Didn't you notice?"

Jason put his arms across his face. "Yeah, I noticed, but it's not fair. You're engaged to another man and I'm going home in a few days."

"Do you have to go home in a few days?"

"Yes, I do."

Sarah stood up and turned away. Jason put his right arm down. "What good would it do if I stayed? You're engaged to Christian."

Without turning around, Sarah inquired, "What if I weren't engaged?"

Jason dropped his left arm with a thud. "But you are, and even if you weren't, what's changed with us?"

Sarah spun around. "You're here. I'm here. That's changed."

Jason answered with forceful conviction. "But, my ministry is still in the U.S, and yours is in Ecuador."

Sarah shook her head and sighed. "But God has brought us together again."

"True, but I don't know why."

Sarah moved closer to the bed. "Jason, do you love me?"

"What good would it do if I did?"

"Look at me. Do you love me?"

Jason refused to look at her. He knew she'd know the truth, and that would only make things worse.

"Jason, please look at me. I have to know. Do you love me?"

"I'd be foolish to love you."

Sarah let out a frustrated breath, and asked the question again slowly. "Do … you … love … me?"

He didn't answer. She bent over the bed and tried to grab his face. He deflected her efforts.

He brought an end to the whole thing. He answered strongly and firmly, "Sarah, I don't love you. You can marry Christian with no regrets. He'll be good for you ."

Sarah stood up and turned away. Jason could tell that she was wiping tears. He felt like a heel. But what was he supposed to do? *Oh God, what do I do? Do I take it back? Do I tell her the truth? What good would it do? We can't be together.*

"Jason, I'm sorry. I thought you loved me like I love you."

He couldn't believe his ears. He sat up in the bed. "What?"

Sarah didn't answer. She turned and hurried out the door.

Jason struggled to get out of bed. "Sarah come back," he yelled. "I do love you. I do."

Chapter 31

But, she didn't come back. Jason grabbed a blanket to wrap around him, and the portable IV pole and headed toward the door. He didn't make it to the door before he collapsed.

———————◆———————

When he came to, Jason was back in the bed and Roy was sitting in the chair beside it.

"Hey there pal. It's good to see you. How are you doing?"

"I'm great."

"I understand you'll be ready to go home in a few days."

"Yeah, I guess."

"You don't sound so sure. What's up?"

"Have you seen Sarah?"

"I saw her out front when I arrived a couple hours ago; she was waiting for a taxi. I asked her how you were doing. She said she knew you'd be okay now."

Jason's eyes narrowed as he shook his head in frustration. "Where is she? Do you know?"

"She said she was going back to Otavalo."

Jason put his arm over his head. "Back to Christian."

"Back to the hospital, anyway. What's going on with you two?"

"I blew it, Roy. She asked me if I loved her and I told her no. I told her to marry Christian with no regrets."

A look of confusion took over Roy's face. "You told her to marry Christian? She hasn't been engaged to Christian since your kidnapping."

Jason sat up in the bed. "What?"

"She loves you, pal. Couldn't you tell that?"

"I guess I knew, but my ministry is in the U.S. and hers is in Otavalo."

"That may have been true in the past, but she's had me searching for a position for her around Kansas City for the last six months."

Providencia — Deborah A. Hodge

"For six months?"

"She never gave up on you being freed. She said that God had assured her that you would be, and that you two would be together. So she started looking for a job in Kansas."

"I don't believe it. God answered my prayers and hers and I was too dumb to know it."

Roy laughed. "Never doubt the providence of God. He's working even if we can't see it and even if we don't know it. Maybe it's just now time for you to know it."

"Roy, I have to see her. I have to straighten things out."

"Why don't we call the hotel and see if she might still be there? If she's not, we'll go to Otavalo as soon as you are well enough."

Jason fell back into bed. His fever was spiking again. He pushed the call button and asked the nurse to come in. "Roy will you call Sarah for me? I have to see her. I have to straighten things out. "

Roy agreed, "Sure, buddy. I'll go make the call."

Cate answered the phone. "Mrs. Barnes, is Sarah there? … She's not … Jason wants to see her … I know she's upset. I know what he told her, but he thought she was still engaged to Christian … No, she didn't tell him … I told him, and he's beside himself. I also told him about Sarah's seeking a job in Kansas … He's determined to see her and straighten things out … Thank you Mrs. Barnes … I appreciate anything you can do. We'll see you later."

When Roy returned to the room, Jason had his eyes closed. Upon hearing the door open, he opened his eyes. "She wasn't there, Jas. She's at the airport waiting for her flight back to Otavalo. Mrs. Barnes said that she'd try to catch her before she left."

Jason nodded and closed his eyes. "Okay, thanks." The medicine took effect and he drifted off to sleep. His fever edged up and he slept a restless sleep until the next morning. He woke up as the nurse poked the thermometer under his tongue. He closed his eyes as she took his temperature. "105, he's had another episode," the nurse reported.

Jason heard her words but couldn't seem to open his eyes. He heard muffled voices as he drifted off again. He shivered, shook, sweated and slept for the next two days. When he finally woke, his eyes wouldn't focus. He suspected he still had fever.

Chapter 37

His half-open eyes were greeted by Roy's cheerful face. "Are you back with us, Jas?"

Jason muttered, "I guess so."

Roy pushed the call button and informed the nurse that Jason was awake. She hurried into the room to check his vitals. "102, fever's still a little high. You need to rest, Dr. Parks."

"We'll see that he does." Jason realized that it was Sarah's mother speaking.

"Mrs. Barnes," Jason said. Cate walked over to his bed.

"How are you?" Cate asked.

"A little shaky, I'm afraid," Jason answered, closing his eyes.

"We've been praying for you," David added.

Jason opened his eyes again. "Thanks, Mr. Barnes."

"We're all here," Luz said.

"Sí," Eduardo chimed in.

"We've been worried about you." Jason realized that was Sarah's voice. "Sarah."

She came closer. "Uh-huh, I'm here."

The compulsion to sleep was taking over again as he repeated in a low, almost inaudible tone, "Sarah."

He slept the rest of the day and night and awoke the next morning to find only Sarah, asleep in a chair beside his bed. He wasn't sure that it wasn't a dream. He rubbed his eyes and tried to open them wider. He raised his head to get a better look. It was her, all right. He lay back in the bed and watched her sleep.

Lord, I thank You for giving me a second chance to make things right with her. You made Your will clear to her; make it clear to me.

As he lay there watching Sarah sleep and contemplating the last year, God's will became clear. If the abduction had never happened, he would have gone back to Kansas and left Sarah behind, convinced they could never be together. The time in captivity had taught him that God is able to sustain His children in all kinds of situations, and that He is constantly

Providencia   *Deborah A. Hodge*

working in ways we do not see or understand. The instigator of his abduction had become a Christian, his emancipator, and a dear friend. That could only be a God thing.

Giving Sarah and his love for her to God five years ago, the unexpected illness that forced him to come to Ecuador, the translator who couldn't translate, Sarah taking her place, Sarah and him being forced to spend time together, her breaking her engagement to Christian, and her seeking a job in Kansas – all these had to be God things. God had been working behind the scenes the whole time and he had missed it. He had always believed in God's Providence. He couldn't believe that he had been so blind to it.

Thanks, Father, for opening my eyes, and thank You for Your faithfulness and Your Providence. Help me to never be blind to it again.

He watched as Sarah stretched and opened her eyes. He greeted her cheerfully, "Good morning."

She abruptly sat up. "Good morning. How are you?"

Jason smiled. "Better, I think."

She stood up, felt his forehead and gently placed the thermometer under his tongue.

"Still feverish, I think." Reading the thermometer, she added. "101, I was right."

With the thermometer out of his month, Jason inquired, "I thought you were in Otavalo."

Sarah brushed his hair from his forehead. "I got bumped."

Jason smiled broadly. "Hm."

"Hm, what?"

"The Providence of God."

"What do you mean?"

"I mean I needed to talk to you, to straighten things out, and God made it possible."

Sarah folded her arms. "What do you mean you need to straighten things out?"

He frowned slightly. "Didn't Roy or your mother tell you?"

With a tight mouth, Sarah nodded. "They did, but I need to hear it from you."

He summoned his courage. "Okay, I handled things very badly the other day."

With arms still folded, Sarah tapped her foot. "You lied to me."

Jason was shocked at her statement but slowly realized that she was right. "I didn't mean to. I thought you were engaged to another man. I thought I was being noble, letting you go again to do God's will."

Sarah moved closer. "The last time you did that at least you were honest with me."

Jason closed his eyes and shook his head in regret. "I know; I'm sorry. I've been blind to what God has been doing, and I was afraid that I was the only one still in love."

Sarah took his face in her hands. He opened his eyes. "You've never been the only one. I told you I love you. I've always loved you."

Jason covered her hands with his. They both drank in the moment. She bent down and kissed him tenderly. He wrapped her in his arms. Joy flooded both their hearts.

"God is so good," Jason rejoiced.

Sarah laughed. "He surely is."

"He has done exceedingly, abundantly more than I could ask or think."

Still in his arms, Sarah reached up and touched his face. "Uh-huh, you're right, and you need to hurry and get well so we can go home."

He shook his head. "Huh-uh."

Sarah cocked her head, narrowed her eyes, tightened her lips, and frowned as she looked at him.

Jason laughed. "I've got to hurry and get better so we can get married *before* we go home."

Sarah smiled and kissed him, rejoicing in the providence of God.

CPSIA information can be obtained at www.ICGtesting.com
Printed in the USA
LVOW06s2001301213

367514LV00001B/7/P

9 780982 049006